The plot thickens. . . .

Celia's exultant laugh rang out, then stopped. Bewildered, the actress shook her head like a puzzled child. She lifted a music box, an integral part of the unfolding plot, from the bureau and a tune began to uncoil itself, faint and haunting.

She lifted the top of the box. And screamed.

For half a second I thought it was part of the script. Then the sharp shock that had jolted through the sound stage struck me, and I knew. With one accord, Josh and I closed in.

Celia cut her scream off and slammed the lid of the box down. She was shaking all over. Another actress, the heroine of *Lust for Life*, ran over and put her arms around Celia. Josh slid the box from her unresisting fingers. He opened it, and we both peered in. I felt suddenly very sick. . . .

**Other Point paperbacks
you will enjoy:**

point

SOAPS IN THE AFTERNOON

Lavinia Harris

SCHOLASTIC INC.

New York Toronto London Auckland Sydney Tokyo

ISBN 0-590-33058-6

12 11 10 9 8 7 6 5 4 3 2 1   3   5 6 7 8 9/8 0/9

Chapter 1

"I don't see how you can waste your time on that stuff," Josh said loftily, raising that eyebrow of his at the television screen. The theme song of *Lust for Life* poured out of the loudspeaker unctuously. Beneath a glittering chandelier, the soap opera's favorite villainess was about to seduce another poor sap.

We were up in my office, formerly my own private sitting room, before that the Webster family room, on a sunny afternoon in early March. Officially, SSW Enterprises, Computer Consultants, was being set up by Sidney Scott Webster, President, and Joshua J. Rivington, III, employee and computer genius extraordinaire. At least that's what was supposed to be going on. What was actually happening was Josh was slouching back in his favorite chair looking supercilious, and Sidney Scott Webster (that's me) was doing a slow burn. The last thing I needed on this particular afternoon was Josh being Male Chauvinist Pig about my TV habits.

"For your information, if it's any of your business, *Lust for Life* is one of the longest-running soaps on the air." I could be lofty, too, though I hadn't yet gotten the hang of that raised eyebrow. "Lots of famous people, including two American Presidents, have watched it. And it just happens to be produced by Jane Palmer Kirby."

Josh was unimpressed. "So who's Jane Palmer Kirby?"

"*Only* the youngest executive and first woman to become a vice-president of a network. And then vice-president of a production company, and also its executive producer. And incidentally my mother's sister, who just happens to be coming to dinner here tonight."

"Oh, *that* Jane Palmer Kirby." Josh's tone altered. He didn't know beans about soap operas, or commercial TV for that matter. But he read the business pages of the papers regularly. Aunt Jane's name appeared there just as regularly. "I suppose that's why your mother's cooking up a storm downstairs."

"Isn't my mother always cooking up a storm?" Mom's a gourmet cooking expert, and has collected recipes everywhere we've traveled with Dad, who's Chief of Staff at the hospital here in Lakeland, New Jersey. Someday, she keeps threatening, she's going to write a cookbook. Today she was whipping up her special Beef Filet Webster, and the combined aromas of mushrooms, shallots, and prosciutto had Josh's nose twitching.

"She doesn't usually break the bank for an ordinary family dinner," Josh pointed out. "But I suppose Mrs. Kirby isn't ordinary family."

"*Ms*. Kirby. She's divorced. And I have an idea this isn't an ordinary dinner, anyway."

Involuntarily, my eyes strayed to Samantha, and Josh saw it. I should explain Samantha's not a person, though it's sometimes very hard to remember that. Samantha's a computer. A one-of-a-kind, SMN Gemini prototype computer, with extra-special features. The ability to be operated by brain waves, for one thing. So far I'm the only person who's managed to learn how to do that, which is why Samantha's just moved into the SSW Enterprises office on the second level of our split-level house. That, and the fact that it was Samantha, in partnership with Josh and me, who caught the computer thieves who were ripping off Dad's research into altered states of consciousness.

All that had happened just two weeks ago, and Josh and I were still dazed from the publicity. "Teen-Age Whiz Kids," and "Computer Detectives," was the least of what the media called us. That's what prompted me to set up this business. Me, not Josh, because while he may be a computer wizard, he's a minus zero when it comes to organization, and a double minus in sensitivity or diplomacy.

He could startle me sometimes, though, with a remarkable sensitivity where I was concerned. He came up behind me now and put his hand on my shoulder. I turned to face him and he took me in his arms. He kissed me sweetly and when he pulled away, he said. "You're worried, aren't you?"

"Yes," I said. "Aunt Jane doesn't usually just call and invite herself at the last minute, like this. She has so little free time, she has to schedule it weeks in advance. But Mom said she called at one o'clock and said she wanted to come out here on the five o'clock train. And she especially wanted to make sure that I'd be here. She said she had some work she might want me to do."

Something struck me suddenly. "One o'clock. That's when *Lust for Life* starts taping. Aunt Jane never misses watching. And she never leaves the studio before taping's finished, not unless she's arranged for it days before. Taping isn't over until at least nine-thirty."

We looked at each other. "Something's wrong with the show, isn't it?" Josh asked. There was a note in his voice that I could not interpret. It was the same note that had been there when he said, "*That* Jane Palmer Kirby," and it got my back up.

"Just because you look down your nose at soap operas —"

"Can it," Josh said abstractedly. He hesitated. "Look, Sidney, I didn't know whether I should mention it or not. There was a gossip item in today's *Wall Street Journal.* The soap company's dumping the ad agency that's been doing its video commercials. And there's a rumor it may dump *Lust for Life.* The polls show it's consistently been losing viewers over the past three months."

"I don't believe it." But my words were hollow. Vague disconnected memories were coming to my mind. Those two days I'd watched *Lust for Life* when I'd been home with a cold right after the computer rip-off case. One of the story lines had turned me off, and another had been, let's face it, boring. And Aunt Jane — come to think of it, clear back to late last summer — Aunt Jane had been uncharacteristically close-mouthed about her work.

Josh saw my face. For once, he didn't rub it in about soap operas being an inferior cultural form. He went over to Samantha and started disassembling her casing.

I stared at him. "What on earth are you doing?"

"Gearing Samantha up. That's why you've been so witchy this afternoon, isn't it, because you're afraid of what you're going to find out tonight? And afraid Samantha won't be ready for serious business? Well, she will be. And I've figured out a way to up her data-processing capacity."

I should explain that Samantha's residing with us now because the high school decided she was too stealable, and her potential far too scary, to have her user-tested any longer in the school computer lab. How she got there in the first place is a long story. Suffice it to say that Dad's research partner, who's also the high school physics teacher, was a service buddy of her inventor. Josh's playing fast and loose with Samantha's innards was definitely not part of the deal. I knew better than to waste time trying to stop him. He couldn't do any harm, anyway, and he was probably going to end up president of the SMN company before he was thirty.

I left Josh to his chips and wires, and went downstairs to tell my mother what he'd said.

Mother's eyes were sober. "I'm not surprised. When Jane gets quiet, the way she's been doing lately, something's always wrong. She's been like that since she was a child." She finished wrapping her stuffed filet in phyllo pastry and looked at me, frowning slightly. "When Jane called, she asked me if I'd been watching her show lately. I didn't know what to say."

"Because you haven't?"

"No. Because I have. And I was afraid she'd ask me what I'd thought. She never asks, but today I was afraid she would."

Something, decidedly, was fishy. I pulled out a chair at the kitchen table and sat down. "The show's been kind of boring lately," I offered tentatively.

"Not boring. Sick." Mother joined me, wiping her hands on her striped denim apron. "I don't know whether what's happening to Celia is supposed to be voodoo, or insanity, or plain old witchcraft, but I don't like it. More to the point, I don't believe it. The writers have spent two years building Celia up as an ideal person. The way they have her now, she'd be an ideal candidate for your father's research. In a padded cell, that is."

Celia, as I remembered, had been Mother's favorite character on the show. It didn't sound like Aunt Jane's kind of story line. Of course, I was no expert on what stories helped sell the sponsors' products. And scary tales were huge successes in paperbacks and movie houses. All the same. . . .

"Come to think of it," I said slowly, "that's what bothered me the last time *I* watched the show. I didn't feel deliciously shivery. I felt kind of sick."

Mother nodded. "I worry about Jane," she said unexpectedly. "All the status trappings, but what has she, really? She isn't getting any younger."

"Mother! You're not trying to say that because she isn't married —"

"Don't put words in my mouth. I mean she's in a glamor industry, and you know what that's like. The more glamor, the less security. And soap operas are a youth-market business."

It seemed queer to think of my Aunt Jane as not being part of the youth market. She's always been — I don't know — ageless. And glamorous. And extremely confident. Everything, in short, that I wanted to be some day. But Mother's words sent a shiver down my spine.

Maybe they wouldn't have, if it hadn't been for Aunt Jane making a point about wanting to talk to me. And the sense I had, growing ever stronger, that it was connected, not just with my free-lance computing, but with Samantha's special features and what Dad and Josh referred to cutely as "Sidney's ESP."

Only this time Josh was showing some kind of ESP of his own. He'd assumed, too, that my aunt was going to need the Computer Consultants' unique services. Josh wasn't usually perceptive about people, only about machines.

The shiver stayed in my backbone while I set the table. Josh came downstairs, announcing that Samantha was operational, and conned an invitation to dinner from my mother. She looked at me questioningly before she offered it, and I nodded. If I was right, having Josh at the dinner table would be useful.

Josh tied on an apron and started to help my mother, talking gourmet shop a mile a minute. I finished the table, put some more wood in the fireplaces, and went upstairs to beautify myself.

The face that looked back at me from the mirror was abstracted. Dad's dark eyes but my mother's shiny brown hair; a tip-tilted nose that I regretted; otherwise, Mother and I had Aunt Jane's good bone structure. But even with rose-colored glasses on I wondered whether a big, important company would take me seriously as an investigator. A big important company like the conglomerate that owned *Lust for Life*, for example.

I didn't have any rose-colored glasses to put on right now, despite the conviction that my important aunt was turning to me for help. I brushed my hair and fastened it back with a barrette, gave a last glance at my heather-colored mohair sweater, and went downstairs.

My father and my aunt were just coming in the door. So Dad had torn himself away from the hospital in time to meet her train, a corner of my mind noted briefly. But the rest of my mind was registering, acutely, the pallor beneath Jane Palmer Kirby's glowing makeup and the tiny lines around those fabulous green eyes. Aunt Jane's hair was red-gold, and her figure was fantastic in black slacks and a dramatic black-and-white, abstract-patterned sweater. *I* knew the red-gold in her hair depended on a little help, and I knew Aunt Jane was five years older than

my mother. Most people didn't, certainly not
Josh, who had clearly forgotten his negative
opinion of soap operas. He was swaggering
forward, hand outstretched in his best one-
business-executive-to-another manner. If
Aunt Jane was amused, she didn't show it.

"I'm glad you're here," she said. "Sidney
might have wanted to call you over later,
anyway."

For a missed-beat instant, there was a
queer little silence. A draft came in from
around the door; it struck the ceiling light
fixture, and the crystal globe gave a faint
ping. Dad cleared his throat.

"Maybe Jane would appreciate going right
in to dinner, if she has business she wants to
talk about later," he said briskly.

We sat in the gracious, candle-lit dining
room, eating Mother's wonderful food and
making small talk, and all I could think was,
*We're being more artificial than the soap op-
eras Josh despises.*

At last Mother set down her knife and
fork, pushed back her chair and said what I
hadn't dared to. "All right, Janie, quit stall-
ing. You've been pushing that same piece of
meat around your plate for the past ten
minutes, and any time you can't eat filet
mignon, something's *really* wrong. So out
with it."

"You always did know me too well," Aunt
Jane said. Her voice shook slightly. She took
a sip of water and said, very calmly, "I'm

probably making you think it's worse than it is. We're having some trouble with our plot lines, and I want to hire Sidney's new company to do some market research on what story lines would have the most appeal for our market right now."

She was starting to sound like a network executive, and I saw Josh's ears perk up. "Is it wise to be guided by what the *market* wants? After all, the average TV viewer has the intelligence level of —"

I gave him a swift kick under the table. He stifled a yelp and shot me a black look. Aunt Jane gave a humorless smile.

"Oh, it's wise, all right. If I want to keep my job, that is. Or even keep *Lust for Life* on the air. I've been given an ultimatum. Institute a major overhaul of story lines and production style within a month, or the show will go off the air or have someone else in charge. And do it before anyone gets killed."

All at once my ESP was back with a vengeance. I could feel my heart hammering. I wet my lips. "You mean before you have to kill off some of the soap characters?" I said carefully.

Aunt Jane shook her head. "I meant exactly what I said. Yesterday there was a fire on the set — a wire short-circuited. And last week Margaret Geller said there was something funny with her coffee. There may have been other things. . . . It's always turbulent on a set when a show is going through a crisis. It's been building for weeks now, even though the sponsors only lowered the boom on me today. A cast and crew can always tell. . . . Only this time, there may be something more. Something dangerous. Something — *sick.*"

Chapter 2

"I've brought you a batch of research materials to get you started." Aunt Jane spun the combination lock on her attache case, then stopped, glancing from one of us to the other. "That is, assuming you will take the case?"

It was half an hour later, and she, Josh, and I were up in the seclusion of my office, my parents having generously suggested we'd want a private conference.

"We'll take it!" Josh and I both said at once. Josh grabbed me around the waist and kissed me hard. I looked at him in surprise — Josh was not given to public displays of emotion — and then I smiled at him. Josh had the grace to redden.

"That is, if Sidney doesn't want it for SSW Enterprises, I'd be glad to — er, see what I can do alone, if you want," he finished lamely. I suppressed a grin. Poor Josh was having trouble getting used to the idea of me as boss. The thought of Josh swimming through a sea of soap opera, with or without me, tickled me. But the expression on my aunt's face made us both sober quickly.

"I want Sidney," Aunt Jane said quietly. "You, too, if you can keep this confidential. I *know* I can rely on Sidney."

"You can trust Josh," I said hastily. "He's a perfect clam. And where research is concerned, he'd keep his mouth shut for the sheer delight of making outsiders suffer. Dad trusted him with *his* secret research, if that means anything."

"That's why I've risked coming to you two." Aunt Jane snapped her case open and took out a bulky computer printout. "A lot of people would give a good deal of money and power to get this."

"What is it?" I asked, putting Josh out of his misery.

"The writers' plot book for *Lust for Life* from when the show first began twenty years ago — up to the present, and including the projected story lines as they now stand for the next six months." Aunt Jane folded her hands on the cover and stared at them for a minute. "The future story lines will have to be changed now, of course, but this will give you a handle on where they were going. You must never, *ever*, tell anyone you've seen this. Or even that you've worked for me. I'll need a written contract to that effect."

There was a moment of silence as this

sank in. "So this really is serious," Josh said respectfully. "I thought —"

"I know what you thought," Aunt Jane said grimly. " 'Soap operas are trashy. Only morons watch them. They probably pull the plot lines out of a basket blindfolded.' Don't kid yourself; soap operas are big business, and the ratings races are as cutthroat as for prime time. So we'll proceed no further with this, kiddo, unless you're prepared to take my work as seriously as you did that computer theft hoopla at your high school."

"I am. We are," Josh said in dead earnest. "I was just surprised that industrial theft could be involved. Or danger."

"There is danger. I'm convinced of it." Aunt Jane took a deep breath. "One of the things I want you to do is get a printout of upcoming scenes that would lend themselves to sabotage." She looked at Josh. "You're good at high tech matters, aren't you? I have a gut-level feeling that if anything happens, our technical equipment will be involved. It makes accidents so plausible!"

"Like the fire on the set," I said. Aunt Jane nodded.

"That's being investigated, of course. I don't want to tell the authorities my own suspicions, unless I have some evidence that they're well-founded."

"But you have reasons to think they are," Josh said shrewdly.

"I'm not going to share them. I want you to come at this with an open mind. That's why I've brought the printouts and the character profiles."

"How did you carry them off if they're so top secret?" I asked curiously. My aunt's mouth twisted.

"There are prerogatives to being the producer. No one sees the plot book except myself, my assistants, the sponsors' representative, and the writers. It's developed several months ahead. My assistant takes our story conference notes down in shorthand, and then transfers them to a computer disk. The head writers gets a printout, and the only other one stays locked in my office. Disks of back story lines stay there too — all the really old ones were computerized the year I came. The current disk goes home to a safe in my apartment. That's where I ran off these printouts, before I caught the train this afternoon."

She must have had a frantic day, and been away from the studio for most of it — something she never did. "Okay," I said briskly, "how do you want us to get started?"

"Read the story lines. All of them, back to the beginning. Tabulate the main ones, the subplots, and how often each has been used. I suspect you'll find plenty of repetition. If you can, chart out how and when each continuing character has been changed."

She reached into the attache case again.

"Here are the current profiles of each character, with the dates that each one was introduced. And here's a record of the weekly ratings share of *every* soap opera on the air, going back ten years. That's as far as I was able to find the records. What I want is to try to correlate plot developments and character changes with ratings shifts." Aunt Jane sat back, looking drained. "In two weeks. Is that possible?"

"With Samantha, here, anything's possible!" Josh said grandly. Statistics always turned him on. "Shouldn't we correlate what other soap operas were doing at the same time? Is there any way to get that information?"

Aunt Jane brought out another piece of paper. "This woman runs a weekly newsletter covering all soap operas. I know her, but I can't have her knowing I need the information. You'll have to think of a cover story, but she can provide you with back issues covering several years."

"Then I guess all we need now is to get started," Josh said happily.

There were a good many unanswered questions in my mind. I chewed them over as a knock sounded on the door and Mother entered, carrying a laden tray. "You must need coffee by now," she told Aunt Jane firmly. "And I'm certainly not going to let you leave without trying this chestnut torte. Speaking of which, there's no reason for you to leave tonight. You can go in on the train tomorrow morning."

Aunt Jane shook her head. "I have to be on the set by five A.M. There's someone that I have to talk to."

There was something about the way she said that. . . . Josh and I exchanged glances. "Scott and I will drive you to the city when you're ready," Mother said, deliberately casual, and departed. Josh went back to his favorite chair. He was leaving the initiative to me. I eyed my aunt.

"What triggered this today, anyway?" I asked at last. "The sponsors didn't lower the boom out of the clear blue sky, did they? Especially if they'd already seen the upcoming plot lines?"

"We've been discussing the need for phasing in changes for some time. I've been trying to bring them about gradually." Aunt Jane stopped. She stretched her arms above her head and then slumped back against the sofa, her eyes closed. Suddenly she didn't look glamorous any more, or young. The sight unnerved me.

"What happened *today?*" I asked again, gently.

She didn't even bother opening her eyes. "The sponsor's representative flew in unexpectedly, to take me out to lunch. Meaning off the premises, so we wouldn't be overheard. Two of our major markets have just dropped the show," she said starkly. "The network affiliates are always free to do that. If it's someplace where the ratings don't matter, then it's nothing. These were Chicago and Philadelphia. They're *not* nothing. So, I got an ultimatum. No more gradual changes. Immediate surgery. Either I do it, or they'll bring in someone who can."

Even Josh looked shocked. "Just like that? No reasons given?"

"Oh, they had reasons," Aunt Jane said tersely. I felt that eerie prickle go up and down my spine again.

"It's that story line, isn't it? Celia and her witchcraft, or whatever it is."

Aunt Jane looked at me oddly. "That's what brought things to a head," she agreed. "The character was introduced last year as part of a short-term story. She wasn't supposed to be in the show this long. The actress playing her has a three-month contract. All our running characters do; that way we can always phase them out if it becomes necessary. Celia was supposed to come on like an angel, become the source of trouble without anyone knowing she was behind it, be exposed as a mischief-maker, and take off for parts unknown."

"What happened?" Josh asked.

"Two things. One, she aroused strong reactions in viewers. People loved her or they hated her. She's artistic. She's a free spirit. She's a health-food nut. She picketed for nuclear disarmament. Some viewers don't like that. Others think she was the best thing that had ever hit River Edge." That was the mythical city where *Lust for Life* took place. "Anyway, she got talked about, and we figured that would probably be good for the ratings, so Celia stayed."

"You said two things," I reminded her.

Aunt Jane sobered. "The other thing was that our head writer fell in love with her own creation. It's always bad when you become so enamored of something you've created that you can no longer look at it objectively. The writer's obsessed with Celia as a weirdo, even though the viewers *aren't*."

Josh frowned. "What can you do when that happens?"

"It depends on how bad the situation is, and on the writer. If the writer is still able to be objective, then the character gets changed. That's what was supposed to be happening, for the past six weeks. But the changes simply . . . haven't materialized substantially enough. Oh, they'd *read* all right, on paper, but on the TV screen it was different." Aunt Jane shrugged. "Of course," she added justly, "I've been trying to make these changes without giving the cast and crew reason to start smelling danger. They're smelling it anyway. Maybe that's why. . . ."

"Why what?" Josh asked quickly.

"Why the studio's starting to turn weird, too. Places can have personalities too, you know, just as people do. Ours has developed a macabre sense of humor." Aunt Jane performed that shutting-off-the-subject trick again, and gave a slight shake that turned her back into brisk businesswoman. "All right, then. You get started processing this raw data. I want a profile of what combinations of story elements have resulted in the highest audience ratings — among *all* soap operas — during the past three years. I'll try to put off our new story conference until I have it."

Despite his opinion of soaps, Josh looked like a kid who'd been given the key to a candy store. I wished I could share his feeling. "You said there had to be immediate surgery," I said slowly.

Aunt Jane grimaced. "Tomorrow morning I have to tell our head writer and one of our best actresses that their services are no longer needed. Leslie has six weeks more on her current contract; we'll dream up a way to phase her character out over that period of time. Leslie never expected the job to last this long, anyway, and she probably has a lot of other offers. It's Margaret Geller I hate facing. She created *Lust for Life*, you know."

That had been twenty years ago. I had an image of a middle-aged woman thrown suddenly out of work. Only if *she* wasn't, Aunt Jane might be. . . . "It's going to be hard on her," I said tentatively.

"Not financially, thank goodness. To tell the truth, she's burned out. She's always been brilliant but erratic. But the past few years, she's been *making* trouble for herself. Insisting on weird plot developments; writing out characters viewers loved, if she suddenly turned against the actors who played the roles. Honestly, I should think she'd be half glad to retire. But not like this, thrown out of something she created." Aunt Jane rose. "Oh, well, it goes with the territory — for both of us."

I hoped it wouldn't for Aunt Jane. I watched her, slim and elegant, pull down her sweater and close her attache case. For the first time in my life I felt sorry for her.

Aunt Jane went downstairs to tell my parents she was ready to leave, and Josh and I sat looking at each other.

Josh cleared his throat. "Okay, I'll take the plot book home with me and start pulling those statistics." Josh always was a night owl, but we both knew my folks wouldn't take kindly to his pulling an all-nighter in my office on a school night. "You and Samantha want to take the character-change statistics? That's right up your alley."

"First we have to write a program for the data bases."

"First we have to agree on exactly what the job is that we've been hired for."

I just looked at him.

"To crunch statistics and come up with a foolproof story line? Or to prove who's fooling around with a plot backstage? Your aunt wasn't exactly clear."

Josh was right. I'd have seen it if I hadn't been so personally involved. "I guess our real objective is to save her job. That's why we need statistics. But they may not be enough if we don't get to the bottom of the sick sense of humor on the set at the same time."

I didn't spell it out. We were both thinking the same thing, even while Josh kissed me good-night gently and took his leave.

Aunt Jane needed those statistics, but that wasn't why she needed us. Josh and I were back in business as detectives.

Chapter 3

The phone woke me the next morning, shrilling while it was still dark. I reached for it sleepily. A call at this hour was usually for Dad, but there was no reason for him to be wakened if it wasn't. He must have gotten back very late from driving Aunt Jane home.

"Hello?" I said sleepily. And then sat up straight, snapping the lamp on as I did so. "Aunt *Jane?*" The hands on my bedside clock stood at twenty to six.

"Just keep quiet, and listen." Aunt Jane's voice sounded very controlled. "I'm calling from the delicatessen up the street from where I work. I came in at five, for the purposes I told you." That meant she'd left her office so the call wouldn't be overheard by any of the *Lust for Life* company, but didn't want outsiders to understand what she was saying, either.

"Something's happened, hasn't it?" I was immediately wide awake.

"Too right, it has. Some work we taped three weeks ago — what was scheduled to be used tomorrow."

That meant the tape for tomorrow's show, I translated mentally. "What happened to it?" I asked.

"You tell me."

"You mean it's disappeared?" I gasped.

"Correct. I've done a total check. Gone with the wind."

"What are you going to *do?*"

"Change the game plan," my aunt said crisply. "What I said yesterday about you being unofficial. Cancel that. I want you both in here as soon as possible, to do the research we discussed. Since I learned about you through the media after your last assignment, you're newsworthy. That may be useful."

. And *that,* translated, meant she didn't want anyone to know we were related. "I think I can spring us both from school this afternoon," I said thoughtfully. "You want us to come in?"

"Yes."

"Aunt Jane, have you told Security about this yet? And the police?"

"Yes. No. I'm about to confer with the person I had lunch with yesterday."

"What are you going to do about tomorrow's show?" The enormity of what had happened struck me. Today's production schedule had to be already tightly packed. "If the tape's not found —"

"Only one thing we can do," Aunt Jane said flatly. "Live."

"You mean a live performance, directly onto the air?"

"That's right. And pray that nothing — *humorous* happens."

She meant *dangerous*. I felt as if all Samantha's circuits were operating full speed in my head. "Aunt Jane — listen. A live performance will get you lots of good publicity, won't it? You said you needed immediate surgery. Why don't you revise the script — have something happen to Celia at the end of it? It wouldn't matter what. A car crash. A gun going off. Her falling out a window. You wouldn't have to show why, or how. Just ... *end* her. You said your head writer's been doing things like that already. You'd have all that transition time with your new head writer to develop and solve the mystery. It would end the current story line in a hurry, with a mystery. And if you can get lots of publicity lined up for the live broadcast, you should attract loads of viewers." One thing I was sure of, even without statistics: Crime in a TV show always hooked an audience.

Aunt Jane was silent so long I was afraid I'd gone too far. When she did speak, there was a new note in her voice. "You're onto something. I *was* right to hire your company, and I'm going to use that as a sales point in my next call."

Which meant the sponsor was going to hear all about SSW Enterprises, and SSW Enterprises would probably get a lot more publicity. My rational mind was enchanted. The other part of my mind was too busy being conscious of cold chills up my spine. Tapes of TV shows didn't just disappear. They *couldn't* just disappear — not unless it was engineered by somebody professionally involved. And not unless it was for some very serious reason.

"I'll expect you both shortly after lunch then," Aunt Jane said in her executive voice. "I'll arrange for visitor passes to be waiting, and my assistant or someone will come down to meet you. It's been good talking to you, Miss Webster." She hung up.

I called Josh's apartment and got him out of bed. Josh whistled. "I thought something might happen, but not this soon. Has she fired those two dames yet?"

"She didn't say. Anyway, the tape was already missing when she got there, so there couldn't be any connection. Meet me by my locker, will you? We'd better tackle the principal together."

"I'll be there twenty minutes early," Josh said, and hung up.

I hadn't had a chance to tell Josh we'd have to put on the Big Business front, but it didn't matter. Josh always dressed like a business executive. I contemplated the subject of what clothes would make me look like the president of a computer company, then went downstairs to break the news about all this to my parents.

They were at the kitchen table, wreathed in the tantalizing aromas of apple upside-down coffeecake and coffee. They both looked sober, and they looked even more so after they'd heard my tale.

"Of course you can leave school early. I'll write you a note." Dad pulled out, of all things, a prescription pad. "I must admit I was hoping you'd have a spell of being an ordinary schoolgirl before plunging into any more high-powered computing." He *said* computing; he *meant* detecting, and we all knew it. Mother did not look thrilled.

"If it wasn't Jane . . . if she wasn't in such a spot. . . ." Mother pulled herself together. "I'm just glad she wasn't too proud to ask you two for help," she finished firmly.

"So am I. Mom, what do I tell my friends? There's a lot of this that's not supposed to get out. The kids know Aunt Jane, and she doesn't want the people at the network to know I'm her niece."

"Tell them you got a call to do some data processing for the network on the strength of all that publicity from Project Aardvark." That was the name of Dad's research which Josh and I had saved from being stolen. "If Cordelia puts two and two together, tell her you don't want people thinking nepotism's the only reason you got the job."

Dad laughed. "I don't think you have to worry. Cordelia will probably be too enthralled by TV glamor, and Ceegee and the other computer jocks too enthralled at the prospect of maybe being brought in for some free-lance computing jobs, to be looking between the lines for a mystery."

That proved a very accurate assessment.

Early as I tried to slip out of the house, Ceegee, a.k.a. Charles Gordon Richardson, came loping from next door as soon as I started down the path. "What are you duded up for?" he inquired, taking in my high heels, pinned-up hair and Mother's borrowed cashmere coat. "Hey, did you get a job? Anything in it for me?"

Ceegee looks like a tall scarecrow, has lived next door for practically forever, and I love him like a brother. Fortunately, since Josh and I got together, he has settled back into seeing me as a sister. A younger sister whom he knows all too well.

"It's a job. In New York. There might be some statistical work in it for you, I don't know yet. Oh, there's Cordelia!" I said in bright relief. Cordelia Quinn is my dearest friend and *not* a computer freak. She also checked out my clothes, gave me a shrewd look, and in response to my unspoken plea launched into a totally different subject.

"Steve and I are going to that rock concert

over in Highview Saturday night. You guys want to join us? Ceegee can dig up a date somewhere, can't you?"

"I don't know how Josh will react to a rock concert," I said cautiously. Aunt Jane's work could tie us up all weekend anyway.

"That's what you get, dating a highbrow," Ceegee jeered. Cordelia tossed her long dark hair and her eyes sparkled.

"It's better than dating a computer jock, take it from me!"

Ceegee, Cordelia's boyfriend Steve Wiczniewski, and their pals were all athletic stars and hooked on hacking. Hence the computer jock appellation. I may be president of a computer company, but if you call me a hacker, *smile*. Josh, should anyone be so mistaken as to imagine him a jock, would probably avenge the insult with a karate chop. As for Cordelia, she thought computers were boring, period.

"If I have to listen one more time to you and Steve rhapsodizing over the additional speed you get from hooking the whoozidink up to the gizmo —!" she was telling Ceegee now. That argument, blessedly, lasted us until we reached the school, where I was able to ditch the others before meeting Josh.

I filled Josh in quickly on what I hadn't covered on the phone. Josh, darn him, started looking happy.

"It's gone beyond — what did your aunt call it — a sick sense of humor? Swiping a not-yet-broadcast TV tape has to be related to hard business facts. Ratings. Money. This is something we can get our teeth into, much better than backstage spooks and all that garbage." Josh always was more comfortable when he could avoid having to deal with the irrational.

"I don't think the kind of malignant tension Aunt Jane was talking about is garbage," I said acidly. "How are you making out plowing through the plot book?"

Josh winced. "You don't want to hear. The principal should be in his office by now, shouldn't he? Let's go do our sales job."

It wasn't too difficult. Josh and I both have Monahan's computer class in the afternoon, and though it would kill him to admit it, Monahan's our buddy. The principal, once he'd gotten over being flabbergasted at the explosions Josh had rigged Samantha to set off in the computer classroom during our last case, had been very relieved that we'd caught two criminals by doing so. He was willing to count the work SSW Enterprises did for Aunt Jane as part of the school's work-study program.

By twelve-thirty we were on a train for New York. By one-thirty we were entering the drab warehouse that was home to the network studios for *Lust for Life*.

I could see out of the corner of my eye that Josh looked stunned, and it tickled me. Here he was in his three-piece pinstripe, his trademark boots, and carrying his attache case. And we were going into what looked like a condemned warehouse in a ramshackle part of Chelsea. He'd undoubtedly been expecting something like the streamlined smoked glass of CBS headquarters uptown. I had a bad minute wondering if the elderly guard would recognize me from the last time I'd been here, two years ago. But he didn't; high heels, hair up, and makeup made a lot of difference.

"Ms. Kirby said you'd be coming," he said, reading our writing upside down as we signed into the visitors' book on the worn vinyl counter. *Name — Time of Arrival — Whom Visiting — Company Affiliation*, the columns asked. I signed *SSW Enterprises*, for the first time, with a flourish.

The guard reached for the phone, and mumbled into it, and Josh and I sat on a shabby green leatherette banquette and twiddled our thumbs. Presently a tall, attractive young brunette, in pants and a sweater reminiscent of Aunt Jane's, appeared.

"You the people from SSW Enterprises? I'm Linda Partridge, Jane Kirby's assistant. She's in a conference right now, but she said I should show you around. We're having final run-throughs on the sound stage. You can watch, if you'd like, until the director's ready to tape, and by that time Jane will probably be free."

Linda was already leading us past the guard's counter, around a corner, and through a maze of canvas flats to a flight of stairs. This place really *was* a warehouse. I saw Josh surreptitiously brushing dust off a trouser leg.

Linda didn't look too much older than I am, I decided. When we went through the fire door at the top of the stairs we saw a couple of very young secretaries, and two actors I recognized who had more wrinkles up close than they did on screen. I guessed we could stop worrying about anyone's speculating on our ages and, therefore, our purpose. Probably everybody in the industry was trying to be either older or younger than they really were.

We were in the small, definitely unglamorous area that was the entrance to everything. A young man sat on another green banquette, looking determinedly calm and hopeful . . . probably waiting to audition for a role. Props and furniture were piled everywhere. *Celia's kitchen — Brannigan apt. — nurses' lounge* was painted like graffiti across the back of a refrigerator. The two middle-aged actors and a fiftyish technician in a gray coverall lounged around a steaming coffee pot. They were joined by an authoritative, quietly dressed woman with a streak of silver in her hair and fine dark eyes. Not one of the regulars in the show. I wondered who she was. Josh was uncharacteristically silent. Over the fire doors to the sound stage a red light was blinking.

"Something's being taped. We can't go in until it's over. You can sit on anything around that's sittable. Coffee?" Linda asked. I shook my head.

Josh seated himself on the far end of the green banquette, his attache placed precisely on his knees. I found a corner of the couch from the *Celia's house* set and perched myself on it. Linda excused herself briefly and we sat in silence. I began to feel what Aunt Jane had spoken of . . . a gray tide that was half tension and half fear, rolling in.

The red light went out. The actors straightened their ties. The technician looked at us and said, "You can go in now, if you want to." And Josh and I followed the actors through the door onto the main *Lust for Life* sound stage.

I say stage. It wasn't. It was a huge cavernous space, a cross between a loft and warehouse. Along every wall, as though they were model rooms, ranged the sets. The district attorney's office . . . the Brannigan living room . . . the hospital nurses' station . . . Celia's bedroom. Above everything ran a catwalk, and a sort of balcony, and from high up, ringing the whole space as though to make a floating stage-set in mid-air, hung panels and panels of curtains and draperies. From the center of the ceiling hung lighting bars strung with stage lights, and more lights were mounted on poles scattered through the open areas below.

"Watch your feet," Linda whispered to us, reappearing. The floor was a treacherous net of lines and cables. They led to lights, to microphones, to cameras that were mounted like grotesque robots on rolling stands. Josh was inspecting them, impressed.

"Stay behind!" somebody shouted at him. "We're trying to check a camera angle!" Josh beat a hasty retreat.

In the shadows of the currently unused nurses' station, two actresses were rehearsing lines in whispers. A few people stood, in twos and three, around the edges of the main area, watching or preparing for entrances. The main focus was down at the far end of the sound stage — Celia's room. The cameras and lights were aimed there, and the man in the beret who had yelled at Josh was conferring with a suited young woman with a clipboard.

"Daniel Wageman. He's today's director," Linda whispered. "The girl's Liz Rayburn, his assistant." I was wondering how Aunt Jane had explained our presence, when Linda volunteered the answer. "I understand you two are going to be doing statistical story line research for us. I'm glad. We can use it."

And just what do you mean by *that*? I wondered silently.

A makeup crew moved in, powdering people's foreheads, adding blusher. Other actors, apparently not in the current scene, began drifting to the perimeter of the set. In the middle of it all, one figure sat silently. She was slight, around my size, wearing a coffee-colored satin slip. An embroidered Chinese robe trailed over the end of the bed. The figure's legs were tucked up under her, and her head was averted, but I knew who she was. *Celia* . . . the character Mother and Aunt Jane and I had been discussing. Or, rather, the actress playing Celia, whom Aunt Jane had to fire.

I wondered if Aunt Jane had done so, yet. She must have, if she really was planning to film Celia's death, live tomorrow. But it was borne in on me, slowly, that amid all the rolling tide that I had sensed swirling and eddying through the sound stage, there was one still center, one person unaffected. And of all unlikely persons, it was this young actress who played the possession-wracked Celia so chillingly.

"Places, please!" the director's assistant called. "One. Two." Celia and the male character with whom she had a love-hate relationship began to move. He blended in, looking down at her. Slowly, provocatively, her head turned toward him; turned up. Her eyes were challenging. In one convulsive movement, they were in a clinch. Then he jerked away. For a moment they stared at each other. Her muscles seemed to gather themselves like a cat's beneath the coffee satin. One hand flashed up, raking fingernails across his cheek, leaving red streaks. He pulled free and flung himself out of the room as she looked after him.

The door slammed. Her exultant laugh rang out. Then stopped. Bewildered, Celia shook her head like a puzzled child. She unfolded herself from the bed; moved to the bureau. Lifted a carved box that I knew to be her grandmother's music box and an integral part of the unfolding plot. Celia's finger pushed a lever, and a tune began to uncoil itself, faint and haunting.

She lifted the top of the box. And screamed.

For half a second I thought it was part of the script. Then the sharp shock that had jolted through the sound stage struck me, and I knew. With one accord, Josh and I closed in.

We got through to the set because everyone else was so preoccupied with what was happening. Celia cut her scream off and slammed the lid of the box down. She was shaking all over. Another actress, the heroine of *Lust for Life*, ran over and put her arms around her. Far across the sound stage, a work light caught a glint of copper. Aunt Jane was hurrying in.

Josh, contrary to all union rules, slid the box out of Celia's unresisting fingers. He opened it, as I edged up and felt suddenly very sick.

In the box, feet folded neatly, was a dead rat with a red cord tied around its neck.

Chapter 4

After that, everything happened fast. A large man whom I'd seen supervising props swept the music box out of Josh's hands with a growl. Aunt Jane and a medium-sized, slightly balding man in a pinstriped suit came running over. The woman with the silver streak in her hair got to Celia first.

"Celia . . . Oh, my dear, how terrible! But you mustn't let it upset you."

"I'm not upset," the actress playing Celia interrupted evenly. "It's all right, Margaret. It simply startled me."

"*Startled* you? I should think so! It's evil, that's what it is, evil. To think —"

"Thank you, Margaret. I appreciate your coping, but I'll take over now." Aunt Jane was very matter-of-fact. Celia, and others too, looked relieved. Margaret? The head writer Aunt Jane had talked about was named Margaret, wasn't she? I remembered what my aunt had said about her being obsessed with the character of Celia, and wondered if it was carried over to the actress playing the role, as well. The actress took a deep breath, the older woman moved away, and everyone's attention shifted as Jane Palmer Kirby, executive producer, took stage center.

She didn't even lift her voice. She didn't have to. It was pitched precisely and it was very, very commanding.

"Thank you all for your good sense in dealing with these manifestations of someone's immature sense of humor. I want you to know that steps are already being taken to bring these — practical jokes — to a halt. Mr. Doyle and I have been discussing remedies just now." She indicated the balding man. "As soon as we can, we'll tell you as much as possible about those plans and how they'll be implemented. Right now, we would appreciate your being the professionals you are, and continuing as if nothing had occurred."

"Professional!" I heard someone mutter. "Somebody around here doesn't know what that word means."

Aunt Jane chose not to hear. "I need not add that stunts of this sort are not in line with our usual working climate. Whoever thinks they are acceptable is not acceptable to me. Mr. Shea, may I have the box and its occupant, please? Use the back-up box for the rest of today's shooting. Miss Webster,

Mr. Rivington, please come to my office. Mr. Wageman, the taping's in your hands."

She took the music box, rat and all, and strode out. Josh and I and Pinstripe started after her like the tail of a kite.

"Okay, places!" the director snapped.

"Just a minute, Dan. I've got an announcement of my own." Tom Shea folded his arms, surveyed the assembled multitude, and bellowed. "Hear this, you wise guys! No props are supposed to be touched except by card-carrying members of our Local or the actors when using them in a scene! Any more props get touched by unauthorized persons, and we walk! And when I find the clown that's been tampering with things, I'm going to bring him up on charges before his union! Or hers!"

He stomped off, chewing on his cigar.

The tail of the kite completed its exit.

Aunt Jane's office was the one closest to the entrance area, a small room both serene and dramatic. Cinnabar red walls made a glowing contrast to the black and gold, vaguely oriental furnishings. On the shelf of a lacquered breakfront, a small TV set soundlessly showed what was now going on on the sound stage, but nobody was looking at it. Josh and I sat gingerly on the paisley sofa, Mr. Doyle folded himself into a side chair, and Aunt Jane threw herself into the peacock chair behind the desk, looking boiling mad.

"Jack, these are the researchers I spoke to you about. Miss Webster, Mr. Rivington, this is Mr. Doyle, the sponsor's representative, who fortunately happened to be in town today."

"Call me Jack," the representative invited, extending his arm for a handshake, first to me, then Josh. He looked pleasant and also clearly worried.

"Jane's told me your recommendation about killing Celia off during one of the scenes we have to shoot live tomorrow. Very astute thinking. If your research is turning up an audience-grabber like that already, we're going to get along very well together."

Josh managed to look suave, but he shot me an accusing glance which Call-me-Jack couldn't see. I hadn't told Josh about my brainstorm for getting rid of Celia in a hurry. "So you *are* going to broadcast tomorrow's show live?" he asked.

"Oh, yes. We almost have to — unless we keep the cast and crew here all night for retaping, and that *would* make the unions scream. As Miss Webster pointed out, we can get a lot of mileage out of a live broadcast. We have the publicity staff alerting all the news media and entertainment press already, and we've inserted announcements into all of our shows today. The network's seeing that announcements are made on prime time shows tonight, as well." Jack Doyle looked considerably happier. "It should be a shot in the arm for the show."

"It will be, once it's successful," Aunt Jane said tartly. Mr. Doyle had been taking the enormity of live broadcasting very lightly.

"Everybody looked awfully calm, considering," Josh said thoughtfully. Mr. Doyle frowned.

"Jane, you *have* alerted them to the new game plan, haven't you?" Mr. Doyle asked.

"Considering that we'd just finished conferring about it when the joker struck again," Aunt Jane said pointedly, "I haven't had a chance. After what just happened, I wanted to get this scene taped before handing them another jolt. I'll go out and make the announcement as soon as it's wrapped up."

She shot a glance at the TV screen, where the *Celia's room* scene was progressing smoothly, then turned back to her desk. "Meanwhile, what do we do about this?"

We all contemplated the music box with its very dead occupant.

"Like you said, a joke," Mr. Doyle said uneasily.

"Maybe. Or somebody deliberately breaking up production according to a carefully thought out plan."

The rat, oddly, didn't make me shiver. It didn't look real; it looked like a fake figure from a toy store. Especially with that red silk cord. Something nagged at my conscious-ness, but I couldn't pin it down.

Then it happened. My mind slipped over into what Dad calls "Alpha state" or, in less charitable moments, "Sidney's freaking out." If we must be scientific, I went into an Al-tered State of Consciousness. Meaning I was sitting there on the couch, but I wasn't seeing the rat and the red silk cord . . . it had noth-ing to do with the red silk cord . . . I was wide awake, but at the same time, I was dreaming. And what I saw was myself, watching tomorrow's broadcast.

I saw Celia, on the bedroom set, closing the door after somebody and smiling. A diabolically angelic, thoughtful smile. I saw her turn around slowly, and cross to the music box, as if drawn. She picked up the box, and turned toward the camera, and in the background like a memory there was music playing . . . thin, metallic, familiar music. It had to be memory, because the box wasn't open — yet.

Celia, that smile on her lips, started to open the box slowly. And the box exploded. Everything exploded. There was a loud clap, and a flash of light, and a lot of smoke. And then there was nothing but Celia, lying on the floor. Celia, as dead as the dead rat.

"She's on to something," Josh murmured.

My head began to clear. Mr. Doyle was sitting forward, very much alarmed. Aunt

Jane looked puzzled. Josh looked smug, as though I was a white rabbit he was about to pull from a hat.

"I think I *am* on to something," I said. "A way you can bump off Celia without having to have any other character involved in the scene." I resolutely pushed aside the other possibility that crossed my mind — that what I'd "seen" could have been an ESP reading of somebody's sick mind, making plans.

When I told the others what I had come up with, they thought I was on to something, too.

"And without having Samantha here, either," Josh murmured with paternalistic pride. I kicked him in the ankle.

"Samantha? Who's Samantha?" Mr. Doyle asked. I could see salary-per-hour figures rushing through his head.

"SSW Enterprises' primary computer," Josh said smoothly. "Ms. Kirby may have told you, one of our service's special features is our state-of-the-art technology. Miss Webster has a long-distance connection to its data bank."

Mr. Doyle, to my relief, was ready to swallow that. There were enough creepy things going on today without bringing up my ESP. He shook hands with both of us again. "Okay, it's all set up, you're taking on the market research job. You're already on the job. We'd better get the paperwork completed before I fly back to headquarters."

"I've had contracts drawn up," Aunt Jane said. "All but the fees. We hadn't yet discussed fees."

She and Mr. Doyle both looked at me, and I could feel myself turning red. I hadn't done any computer work for pay yet, except for Dad. Fortunately, Josh had. "I handle contract terms," Josh said blandly. He named an hourly rate that was very close to the three-figure range. "That's per person, of course," he added. "With a rush job like this, we may have to assign additional personnel."

Mr. Doyle didn't bat an eye. "Just get the job done, as fast as possible," he said. He rose, and shook hands again, and picked up his attache case. "I've got a plane to catch. Talk to you tomorrow after the broadcast," he told Aunt Jane, and bolted.

Aunt Jane and Josh and I were alone with the door shut, looking at each other. She went to the TV monitor and switched the volume up loud. "There's no soundproofing here," she murmured.

"Can we take that?" Josh asked, pointing to the box and its occupant.

"If you have to. You can certainly have the corpse! The music box we really need."

"I don't think that will matter." Josh took the rat out, wrapped it in his handkerchief, and deposited it in a plastic bag Aunt Jane found in her desk. He turned the music box this way and that, and I wondered what he was looking for. We were too new at detecting to have gotten into fingerprints yet.

"How many people could have gotten at this thing?" he asked.

"Probably anyone, provided Tom Shea, our head propman, wasn't looking. You heard how he reacts when anyone touches the props that are in his charge. Because of his wrath, we've alway been able to leave things stored wherever necessary — in those canvas bins you've seen, like the ones post offices use for parcels, or piled on shelves or in boxes in the areaway. Not valuables, of course. But these music boxes aren't valuable."

Something occurred to me. "How would anybody know which of the music boxes would be used today?"

"They wouldn't." Aunt Jane was definite. "It's whichever one Tom happens to send out. Unless one had to be prepped ahead with certain objects Celia needs, which was *not* on today's agenda."

So it could have been only by chance that the rat was found today. That is, if the rat was planted while the boxes were off the set. I couldn't quite figure how anyone could have stashed Ratsie offstage, in full view of everyone.

On the monitor, a scene was completed. Actors, staff, and crew began to mill around.

"Come on," Aunt Jane said. "I have to lower the boom."

Josh interred the cadaver in his attache case, and we trooped after her. "Take five!" the director was shouting as we entered.

"Just a moment, please." Aunt Jane performed her gathering-attention trick again. This time, for good measure, she stepped up onto the landing of the *Judson Armitage living room/hall* set staircase. Everyone could see her; everyone grew immediately silent.

"I regret that I must inform you that another trick was perpetrated on us earlier, some time between when the film editing crew left at five yesterday, and six o'clock this morning. The videotape for tomorrow's broadcast has disappeared."

All at once, the very air around us was alive with chills.

"That is, you will recall, the script shot three weeks ago tomorrow." Aunt Jane overrode the growing swell of sound. "Let me reassure you immediately, there will be no all-night taping session. I have conferred with Jack Doyle, and we are agreed there is only one thing we can do. Tomorrow's show will be broadcast live."

This time the swell of sound was louder, but no longer angry. Apprehensive . . . excited . . . definitely enthusiastic.

"I know many of the younger performers

have never played live, unless they've been interviewed on news shows," Aunt Jane said, smiling. "All I can say is, the camera won't eat you — but you'd better know your lines! And remember anything you've ever learned about improvising in case you have to cover fluffs. The scenes that were scheduled for tomorrow will be rescheduled. The assistant producers will provide you with copies of the script and tomorrow's schedule. Cast members needed, who are not here now, are already being called. So is the media. I think I can guarantee you that what we do tomorrow can turn out to be very valuable for us all. Thank you." She started to step down.

"Just a minute, Jane." It was the handsome, fortyish man who played Judson Armitage, one of the leading men around whom the plots of *Lust for Life* consistently revolved. "I think I can speak for all of us in appreciating how well you're handling all these — incidents." There was a murmur of agreement. "But I think we're entitled to know what steps are being taken to put an end to them before someone gets seriously hurt."

"You're right," my aunt said steadily. "One, the sponsors have authorized the hiring of additional security police. From now on, the production premises will have round-the-clock security. Two, Jack Doyle and I have personally spoken to the police. Linda

Partridge is already briefing the detectives who have been assigned.

"Three — and this concerns not only the practical jokes, but the future direction of *Lust for Life* — we have contracted with a statistical research firm to do market research on what story lines, ours and our competitors', pull the largest viewer share of our target audience. Sidney Scott Webster and Joshua Rivington" — she nodded in our direction — "will be here frequently, but even more frequently will be working with computers to develop new directions for *Lust for Life* with guaranteed audience appeal. They will factor into their analysis everything that they research, and everything they observe. It is our intention that the practical jokes will cease, but *Lust for Life* will not."

Another round of applause, though I could see skepticism and alarm on many faces. Josh and I were the objects of many sharp glances, swiftly veiled.

"I will not keep you any more, for I can see Mr. Wageman is anxious to get on with shooting. Leslie, may I see you in my office, please? Tom, I want to see you in half an hour. Miss Webster, my secretary has the contract for you to sign before you leave."

She was gone.

The actress who played Celia followed, and I knew she was about to be fired. I felt awful for her. I felt awful for us, because Aunt

Jane had laid it on the line. We had to pull a rabbit out of a hat. Or, preferably, an Emmy.

As Josh and I made our exits with all possible dignity, we could feel eyes boring into our backs. Not just where story lines and jobs were concerned, but with the "practical jokes" as well, Josh and I had been labeled as snoops and spies.

Chapter 5

We went home in the worst of the commuter rush, so there was no such thing as privacy. Josh used his attache case as a desk and was busy making notes. I couldn't, and that was only partly due to the jolting of the train. I kept seeing Aunt Jane's face as she told the company, with such assurance, that *Lust for Life* was going to go on. I wondered if she'd convinced them. She hadn't convinced me.

After a while the train was relatively emptied out. Josh put his notebook away and we looked at each other.

"You realize one thing, I hope," Josh said at last. "We're never going to get this done alone."

"We have to! Aunt Jane's counting on us, and we've got Samantha —"

Josh brushed that aside. "I'm not talking about how smart we are. It's the time factor. Even with just the story-line analyses, your aunt wants a miracle overnight. Now you've talked her into bumping off a major character tomorrow. Did it occur to any of you that that means all the shows she's already taped to run during the next three weeks are going to have to be altered, too, to eliminate that character?"

I couldn't believe that none of us had thought of that. I stared at Josh, stricken.

"It *was* a bright idea," Josh said, relenting. "Probably the exact right thing to do, given the circumstances. Live show, lots of publicity, and all. You would have seen the complications, if you hadn't been so close to the situation. But it still means a lot of material will probably have to be reshot, with Celia's violent death worked in. Which means those analyses we're doing are needed *now*, not weeks from now."

"You mean . . . call in the hackers," I said slowly.

Josh looked me squarely in the eyes. "Wouldn't *you* be telling *me* that, if I'd signed for the project?" He had me there. "If you weren't so worried about your aunt, you'd be saying so, anyway. I'm not saying I'm thrilled about farming work out, rather than doing it all ourselves. But I've been doing some calculations on the number of computer hours we're talking about. If we bring Steve and Ceegee in to work on the statistics, we could turn some preliminary data on the best plot options over to the writers by the first of the week."

"What writers? Aunt Jane was firing the head one today."

"That's her problem. I'm sure she'll find some writers to call in. Sidney, look." Josh whipped out his pad of figures. "How long do you figure it would take for you to write the database program? You always can do that faster than the rest of us."

I took a very optimistic guess.

"Right. Then we turn the crunching of the past plot lines, and the plots of the competition, over to the hackers. That frees you and me to concentrate on the special stuff. Work that has to be done on Samantha. And finding the practical joker, as your aunt so delicately calls him."

"She doesn't want anybody else to know about the job we're doing," I said doubtfully.

"What she wants isn't as important," Josh said flatly, "as what's apt to happen if the guy's not caught."

There was a note in his voice that made me look at him sharply. "I'm not happy either," I said soberly. "The show tape missing . . . that's very serious. But it's the kind of thing somebody could be hired to do, or somebody directly involved could do it. It's illegal, it's some kind of soap opera industry espionage, I suppose, but it's — detached. But the rat. . . ." Involuntarily, I shuddered.

"I was wondering what you concluded about the rat," Josh said, watching me.

"There was something about the cord that

means something, but I can't remember what."

"Witchcraft," Josh said. "Red silk cords are used in 'bindings' in some forms of witchcraft, and in casting spells. I read that, when I was doing a report for chemistry on how common herbs and household remedies were used in some cults to induce hallucinations."

I had read it in a scary novel I'd dipped into once and blessedly forgotten. Until now.

"And the rat itself," Josh went on with precision. "It wasn't your common, garden variety house rat. It was a laboratory type."

"Meaning somebody has access to a lab, or deliberately went out and bought it. It didn't just die and then get found."

"It didn't just die," Josh repeated. "And it wasn't killed with the cord. That was added afterwards for a fancy touch. Its neck was broken . . . I'd say, manually. That's why I was looking at the thing so carefully. The fur was matted, as if it had been pressed hard, by someone's fingers."

I shuddered, and the train pulled into the Lakewood station.

Josh took my arm to help me down the steps, and he could feel me shivering. "Try to relax," he said softly as he bent down to kiss my cheek. "There's no point putting yourself through seeing things unless it'll do some good. Anyway, that's only my naked-eye opinion. It ought to be checked scientifically."

Josh knew me too well. That's exactly what I was doing, seeing a pair of hands picking up a small live creature, and grasping its head, and twisting — I gritted my teeth. "We can ask Mr. Jorgensen to check it in the lab," I said in as normal a voice as I could manage. He was a high school science teacher, and Dad's research partner.

"For that matter, we can ask your dad. He's a surgeon, isn't he?" Josh slid an arm around my waist. "Come on, I'll walk you home."

"Are you sure you're not trying to hustle another dinner invitation?" I asked shakily.

"If you're coming up with put-downs, you must be feeling better," Josh said firmly, and marched me up the street. We could have phoned for a ride, but I was glad for the chance to work off the shakes before my mother saw me. The cold March air was a relief.

Mother took one look at us and pulled two chairs out at the kitchen table. "Your father's coming home late, as usual. He says don't go to sleep until he sees you. Sit down, Josh. I've tried putting cinnamon in the spaghetti sauce, like you suggested."

"You sound like you expected Josh for dinner," I said.

"I did. Your aunt called. She said you were on your way, and that she's phoning you after she gets home, which might be after midnight. So," Mother concluded calmly, "I figured your souls would need nourishing."

Mother's treatment for nourishing the soul included a fire in the kitchen fireplace, and candles glowing on the polished pine. The spaghetti sauce, however unorthodox, was very good. "All right," Mother said after we'd demolished our second helpings. "What happened? I'm not prying into your case," she was careful to add. "I'm being a mother hen about my sister."

Josh's eyes met mine, and we were in accord. We would run the rat past Dad before we let my mother get wind of it. She has a thing about rodents. "The Marines landed," Josh said calmly, "meaning the sponsor's rep, who's decided he likes us fine. Ms. Kirby's fired her head writer, and that Celia character's going to be blown to bits tomorrow."

"Just a normal day around River Edge," Mother agreed. "By the way, Cordelia called. You absolutely, positively have to phone her right away, even though I told her that could be late."

"We have to call the hackers, too," Josh reminded me.

"I can save you one call. Steve's at Cordelia's, doing homework," Mother put in.

The day those two got homework done when they were together would be the thirty-first of February. I rang Cordelia's house, and not only was Steve there, but Ceegee, too.

"They're helping me with my science project," Cordelia said unabashedly, "and we're planning about the concert Saturday. You and Josh come on over."

"Forget the concert," I said ruthlessly. "We're going to be too busy, and Steve may be, too. Put him on, will you?"

Cordelia started to explode, sensed something was wrong, and got Steve quickly. "We'll be right over," he said. "You want Cordelia, too?"

"No. Yes!" I corrected swiftly. There was a way in which Cordelia could be of enormous help.

Within fifteen minutes, the three of them were up in my office, listening to Josh and me explain our immediate need of their services as work-for-hire. *"Soap operas?"* Steve exclaimed. "You've got to be kidding!" At the same time, Cordelia was looking at me, frowning.

"Lust for Life? Isn't that —"

"It is, and shut up about it," I interrupted. I gave Ceegee and Steve the evil eye. "Stop laughing your heads off, and listen. We're talking hundreds of thousands of dollars of production and advertising budgets here. And by the way, this is all hush-hush. I can't tell you any more unless you take the job. And you'll have to sign these secrecy agreements with your contracts." I hauled out the forms I'd adapted on Samantha's word processor during the short time I'd waited for the others to arrive. They were modeled after the ones I'd signed earlier.

Ceegee's long hound-dog face looked hurt. "We know about trade secrets," he said reproachfully. "Just because we're hackers, you think we ain't got no ethics?"

"Knock it off, the kid's serious," Steve said absently. "What is it you need us for, Sid?"

"A crash data-pull-and-crunch job. It's important, for more than just soap plots, but I can't explain yet. It may mean all-nighters, and it will definitely mean all weekend."

"Saturday night's out. Unless SSW Enterprises is prepared to pay for these." Steve flashed his concert tickets.

"That can be arranged," I said. All of a sudden, three pairs of ears perked up respectfully. Josh mentioned the hourly pay they'd get, and there was a reverent silence.

"For that," Cordelia said thoughtfully, "*I'll* learn computing."

"You won't have to. I have something much more up your alley." I hauled out the bulky printouts of *Lust for Life* story lines. "You've been watching soaps since we were in pre-school, so you must know all the cliches when you spot them. And you skim-read fast enough to devour three romance paperbacks in an afternoon. What we need before anything else is a list of all the basic plots that have been used on *Lust for Life* from the beginning. With the dates they were used. Then they have to be sorted out into categories and sub-categories. I'm getting condensed versions of all the other soaps' story lines, too, but you can start on this first."

"I'll take it home and read all night," Cordelia promised.

"Uh-uh. None of this material leaves this office. By the way, you'd better sign the contracts before we go any further." They did so. I looked around. "You guys can each spare a computer to bring over here for the duration, can't you?" The hackers, I knew, collected computer hardware the way other people collect stereo tapes. And Josh had recently indulged himself in a fancy model SMN that was like a Samantha without ESP.

Ceegee hauled his long length out of the easy chair. "I'll go get old faithful Apple now. You guys want a ride for yours?"

We spent the rest of the evening converting my office into a war room.

At nearly midnight, my father arrived home and threw everybody out. "School tomorrow, kiddies. That being Friday, you can bring sleeping bags and sack out here the whole weekend, if you want to."

When the others had left, Josh produced his music box specimen, and Dad examined it carefully. "I think you're right. Manual strangulation. I'll have it dissected in the lab tomorrow morning, to be sure." He looked at both of us with a very serious expression. "This is getting nasty. I want both of you to be very careful. I'd prefer to pull you off the case, but —"

He didn't finish. He didn't have to. A vision of Aunt Jane rose vividly before us.

I cleared my throat. "I wouldn't quit, anyway," I said. "I'm too much of a stubborn Webster."

"And you're not my father. You can't make me do anything," Josh pointed out, not smart-mouth, just stating the facts.

Dad grinned, still looking sober, and offered Josh a ride home. Josh preferred to walk; there were some things he wanted to think out. I wanted to do that, too, only before I could the telephone call from Aunt Jane came through. She had realized the difficulties Celia's sudden demise was going to create for shows already filmed, and was relieved to hear of the crash work schedule SSW Enterprises has instituted. She also wanted Josh and me to be on location during the whole day tomorrow, a request with which I was in entire accord. More to the point, she convinced my mother to let me miss the whole day of school. It was the tight control in her voice that got to me and Mother.

When Aunt Jane hung up, my mind was a maelstrom. Maybe doing some programming would put my head in order. I booted up Samantha, but her blinking red lights only made me flash back to the warning lights on the sound stage. And the palpable tension. . . .

I took so long without entering a program that Samantha got tired of waiting. Her monitor started winking red and green.

ARE YOU SURE YOU WANT TO TALK TO ME RIGHT NOW? PLEASE ANSWER!

"Josh must be rubbing off on you. You're getting as sarcastic as he is," I said irritably.

DOES NOT COMPUTE, Samantha's monitor flashed smugly. That was one of her all-too-favorite retorts. "Knock it off or I'll unplug you," I said wearily. "I'm too tired for clever repartee."

Then it struck me. I hadn't keyed in my comment. I'd spoken it, as if Samantha was the human I occasionally forgot she wasn't. And Samantha'd answerd. I must have accidently pushed that unlabeled key I hadn't tried before, the one for verbal entries. Samantha'd reacted just as she was supposed to. It gave me an idea.

"You're supposed to be superhuman," I told her. "So why should I wear myself out? *You* can do the thinking things through for me."

I fed her an empty data disk, and dictated some simple programming, which Samantha took down graciously. Then I left her purring to herself and went to bed. Samantha knew how to read my Alpha waves, and when was

Alpha state more normal than when some-body was drifting off to sleep? Samantha's reception range was supposed to be the length of a basketball court, at the very least, so she certainly could take dictation from one room away.

I was being very parapsychological and scientific, but I hadn't factored in one vari-able. The length of time it was going to take me to get to sleep. One minute I was lying in the dark, half awake, half dreaming, the events of the day drifting through my mind like images on a TV screen. The next I was sitting upright, wide awake, and the light of the March dawn was filtering through the windows.

I dashed into the office, not knowing in what condition I would find Samantha, who could get temperamental about being left unattended.

She was still running, like a cat in slumber, purring to herself. I looked at the monitor for the expected flippant message, and a cold finger touched my neck.

Samantha hadn't been idle, left to her own devices. She'd been reading my Alpha waves while I slept. The stream-of-consciousness data on yesterday's taping was all recorded, and after it Samantha's conclusion.

DANGER ANTICIPATED.

Chapter 6

Josh and I were on the train to New York at an ungodly early hour. Josh was carting his latest toy, a book-sized microcomputer bought out of his earnings on the research rip-off case. "I might as well put any notes right on a cassette instead of making them by hand."

"Besides, your handwriting looks like chicken scratches," I teased.

"Show some respect, woman! Every real executive has an illegible scrawl, the better for safeguarding secrets. You really ought to work on yours," he added kindly. "Right now, anybody beyond the age of six can read it."

We were being silly because we both were worried. Josh's eyes were red-rimmed, and I had to cover up the purple smudges under my eyes with makeup.

We got to the studio as the first shift of cast and crew was checking in. People in jeans and sweaters, looking anything but glamorous, nodded to us. But their eyes were wary. Only the actress playing Celia, of all people, came over to say hello.

"Here to watch our trial by fire?" she asked, smiling.

"I'm sure it won't be that," I said politely.

Josh got that alert, terrier look of his. "You're expecting fire?"

Celia did a double take. "Not literally. I was talking about the live broadcast."

"You don't look very worried."

"I'm not. I grew up in summer stock — a new live stage show every week. Lots of us did; that's probably why we can cope with a new script every day." She glanced around and lowered her voice. "You mentioned fire. I was here when the episode in the technicians' room took place. Maybe we could go out for coffee later."

"We'd like that," I said instantly.

We reached the top of the stairs and she vanished toward the dressing rooms with a wave. Linda Partridge came to claim us.

"We've cleared some work space for you in one of the dressing rooms. Not large, and not with other offices, but at least you'll have privacy."

She led the way down the carpeted corridor past the framed renderings of sets and the montages of cast members past and present. Jane Palmer Kirby's office door was closed. In other offices, secretaries were already typing and designers were already bent over drawing boards. "The crisis call's gone out," Linda said, following my glance.

The cubicle she ushered us into was small, but it was next to the Green Room, or actors' sitting room, and just around corners from both the film storage room and designers' offices. It had two chairs, a wide counter down one long wall, and a closed-circuit TV monitoring the sound stage. It was also soundproofed. "So if actors want to run lines aloud they won't disturb each other," Linda explained.

Josh looked at me. The soundproofing, and the thick carpet in dressing rooms and corridors, explained how somebody had found it so easy to creep around, planting nasty tricks undetected.

"I wonder if there's a way we could rig up some angled ceiling mirrors to see around corners," I said when she had gone.

"Not with these low ceilings. We could on the sound stage. Or set up some concealed video cameras, like stores do to catch shoplifters. I'll talk to your aunt. We can't bring the tech crew into it unless they're first cleared of suspicion. I could rig them myself if it wouldn't make trouble with the unions."

"If we're going to do much more detecting, maybe you ought to try to pass the exams for some union cards."

"Don't laugh. I've thought about it." Josh scanned the facilities of our new office, checked the views out the door. "Have you given any thought to bringing Samantha here?"

"That reminds me." I hadn't yet told Josh about my Alpha-while-asleep dictation, but I did so now. Josh looked suitably impressed.

"I have to have a try at Alpha myself. Did you bring the printout?"

"It wasn't necessary," I muttered, turning pink. Samantha had read a few things about him in my mind that I decidedly did not want him to see.

Josh decided against leaving his baby computer in the cubicle, even though the door was provided with a lock. "If we do bring Samantha, I'll get a special pick-proof lock that will clamp onto the door frame. I've seen them in surveillance equipment catalogs," he said.

For someone who a month ago had scorned detective stories as much as he did soap operas, Josh was certainly getting turned on to our new career field fast.

There being nothing particular to observe along the dressing room corridor, we took ourselves back to the main arena, glancing surreptitiously through any open doorways as we did so. Nobody was in the Green Room yet. Jane Palmer Kirby was known in the industry for running a tight ship and adhering strictly to a well-thought-out schedule. I gave Josh the benefit of my knowledge as we walked along.

"First a scene is blocked. That means the director and actors figure out all the moves and how they'll coordinate with the dialogue. They don't need to tie up the sound stage doing that. They're booked into a small rehearsal room. After that the actors go to makeup. Then they wait somewhere until they're due for a run through."

"In the Green Room?" The lingo was something else Josh was learning pretty fast.

"Only the by-day actors, the walk-ons, and the under-fives." I forestalled his misinterpretation. "Not little kids, though sometimes actresses with babies bring them and a nurse along and set up a day care somewhere. Under-fives are actors with less than five lines of dialogue. Producers like to keep small parts to that limit, because the AFTRA pay scale's lower for them than for performers who have more lines to learn. . . . Like I was saying, actors who have running roles and private dressing rooms usually do their waiting there."

"Or around the coffee pot," Josh added, smiling. We had reached the props dump/entry area, and as before a few familiar faces were gathered around the coffee maker with crew people.

Just as downstairs, there were glances in our direction which were quickly turned away.

"I don't like it," Josh said.

"What? Being snubbed? Poetic justice,

isn't it?" I asked wickedly. When Josh, with his three-piece suits, one lifted eyebrow and disdain for anything not intellectual, had enrolled in our school a month ago, he had acquired an instant reputation for looking down his nose. (A month ago — was that all it was? There were times — like when he walked me home last night — that that scarcely seemed possible. . . . I dragged my mind back to nonromantic matters hastily.)

"I don't mean attitudes. I mean locations," Josh said, fortunately unable to read my thoughts. "Remember that bit about somebody thinking the coffee tasted funny? If it came from that pot, it would be awfully easy to doctor it undetected."

Another location for a hidden camera.

Nothing was being rehearsed on the sound stage yet, but Tom Shea and his crew were busy setting up. Camera and sound people were checking their gear. Aunt Jane was still invisible. Josh turned to me. "Sit in on some blocking?"

"We'd get shot if we tried it. *Nobody's* allowed to watch a blocking." We chose seats in the unused *Nurses' Station* set, and proceeded to make ourselves invisible.

By now, various office personnel were arriving for work. They came, Aunt Jane had said, any time between eight and nine a.m., unless there was some particular crisis going on. Today, I thought, could well fall into that category. The production coordinators and one secretary said hello. Tom Shea grunted in our direction. A heavyset man I hadn't seen before came over.

"You're the people from the research service, right? Jane told me you'd be here. I'm Jake Fisk, the producer for today's opus."

"Did you produce the original episode, three weeks ago?" Josh asked.

"Fortunately, yes. Otherwise there would have to have been a frantic reshuffling of schedules for today. Excuse me, I have to see how Wageman's making out with rehearsing."

So there *had* been some fast reshuffling. According to Aunt Jane, as Josh reminded me, directors alternated days on duty. Wageman must have been called back today especially.

I was not terribly surprised to see Linda Partridge deftly intercept Mr. Fisk before he reached the studio where rehearsal of the rewritten final scene of today's live broadcast was taking place.

The sound stage on which we were ensconced shortly became feverish. It was apparently going to be a double-duty day. Certain scenes previously scheduled to be taped — the ones in which Celia neither was mentioned nor appeared — were still going to be done. A big notice near the mail boxes announced that others (the Celia ones, though the notice didn't say so) would be "rescheduled at intervals next week." Meaning, of course, after fast rewrites could be done! It was dawning on me just what a major task the instant elimination of Celia was creating.

Josh was getting restless. "Call me when something interesting happens," he muttered, and disappeared in the direction of the technicians, where he proceeded to make himself as much of a pest as they would permit. Presently I saw him in animated discussion with the lighting engineer, who then led Josh over to shake hands with the light designer. When I sauntered over I heard snatches of an enthusiastic discussion of the use of computerized lighting boards, and grinned. The possibility of Josh's getting to install surveillance cameras was looking good.

I went back to my bench and started making notes.

"Are you making sense of all this?"

I looked up, startled, covering my notes. The actress who played Celia had sat down beside me. "We've never met properly. I'm Leslie Swayne."

"Yes, I know." She looked weary; her makeup barely concealed the circles underneath her eyes. But again, as yesterday, she was remarkably free from tension, and that puzzled me. She glanced around and lowered her voice even further.

"You took the rat away with you, didn't you? What did you find out?"

"How did you know?" I parried.

"Because I asked Tom if I could have it," she said calmly.

I couldn't help it; my jaw dropped. "It certainly doesn't seem to have bothered you — after the first shock," I said at last.

"My husband's a biologist. I put up with worse than rats when we were in college. I wanted the rat so he could check it out. What did you find?"

So she had taken for granted we'd had it looked at. I decided a shock tactic warranted revealing evidence. "The rat was a lab specimen, not wild. It was strangled, *not* with a silk cord, probably manually."

She didn't bat a lash, but her eyes darkened. "You're wrong about my not being bothered," she said quietly. "I don't mean by the suggestions of voodoo, or of 'Poor Leslie, freaking out like Celia has; the character's rubbing off.' "

That was a rumor I hadn't heard, and I blinked. "Oh, yes, that's on the grapevine. It's the kind of speculation that does crop up at times like this. The tension, I mean. Once in a great while, it's true. I don't mean real 'possession,' " she added quickly. "But when you're playing really traumatized characters, you do tend to find yourself taking them home with you. What worries me is what's going on with the mind of whoever's *behind* these — jokes."

"You don't think they are jokes."

"No, I don't. Neither does anyone else, including Jane Palmer Kirby."

"You wanted to tell us something about the short-circuit that caused the fire, didn't you?" I asked abruptly.

"It wasn't a short-circuit. Not in the usual sense —"

"Leslie!" Dan Wageman called. "We need you!"

"I'll finish later," Leslie murmured, hurrying off.

The morning ticked by, much as yesterday had. The tension built. *Armitage mansion . . . Judson Armitage living room. . . . The Pub . . . the hospital . . .* scene after scene was set up, rehearsed in, put away. I didn't want to distract anyone by rattling scripts, so I tried to guess which scenes were for today's show and which were for taping I'd already noticed that the scripts distributed yesterday contained a final scene that went only up to Celia's reaching for the music box — not the explosion.

Shortly before lunchtime Josh emerged, looking what for him was starry-eyed. "Those technical fellows I've been talking to are great. They're letting us put up hidden cameras. I didn't have to give reasons. They assume it's part of what Ms. Kirby said we would be doing."

"Let's hope one of them's not the joker," I said darkly. "He might sabotage the set-up!"

"I though of that. I'm going to check the installation," Josh said, "*after* they do the work. What have you found out?"

"That Leslie — that's Celia — is used to lab specimens and wanted to take this one home. And is worried the joker's not quite sane. Also that she's not the least bit upset about her character being dealt with."

"She's an actress. She could be putting on an act."

"I'd have felt the vibrations," I said with dignity. "By the way, there's a rumor going around that her character's been rubbing off on her. Someone either thinks she could be the joker, or *wants* that thought. *And* she doesn't believe the fire happened the way it's been reported. She didn't get to explain what she means."

"We'll pin her down during lunch break," Josh said firmly.

Only we didn't get to, because lunch break turned out to be a haphazard affair. Linda Partridge appeared to tell us she was sending out to a Greek deli and what did we want. Ms. Kirby and Leslie Swayne were going to be eating in the executive office with Mr. Doyle, who was flying back in to watch the afternoon's live broadcast. Josh said he'd prefer to take up the technicians' invitation for him to join them at a neighborhood joint.

"There's not much more I can accomplish here right now," he said when Linda left. "I'm going to cut out after lunch and pick up the data on the other shows from that newsletter outfit."

"Don't let them know why!"

"What do you take me for? I'm going to tell them I'm interviewing their publication for writing up in my own financial news service, since soaps are such big business!" Josh straightened his jacket and departed.

I ate my Greek salad and pita in the set designer's office with the designer, the wardrobe coordinator, and the gracious lady who played Caroline Armitage, the matriarch of *Lust for Life.* She was so charming, and so genuinely interested in my work, that I shortly started feeling like a heel. I steeled myself to remember she was a suspect, too.

I worked the conversation around to the fire, and was relieved to find she had not been on call that day. That, at least, could be easily checked. I'd better get call sheets for all the days any incidents occurred, I thought.

The routine of run-through dress rehearsal taping continued until ten to two. Then a final run for today's live performance began. It was different from the other rehearsals, which were in out-of-order segments. *This* swept from prologue through to the final (or almost final) moment, moving directly from set to set as cameras wheeled swiftly, silently. Aunt Jane and Mr. Doyle were up in the control room, and no watchers were allowed on the sound stage. I was shepherded into Aunt Jane's office to watch on the monitor there. Margaret Geller joined me.

"It's terrible it came about this way, but this is an exciting moment of broadcast history, all the same. I'm glad to be a part of it."

"I thought you might have preferred it wasn't today," I said deliberately. This time shock tactics didn't work. Ms. Geller just looked at me.

"So you've heard I'm retiring. I hope the rumor hasn't traveled far. I don't want to announce it until after the broadcast, so no one will be upset. But I'm tired," she said flatly. "I've been in this business thirty-five years, and that's a lot of scripts. I'm taking a year off to travel, perhaps write my autobiography. After that, we'll see. I have a cottage in the south of France I haven't been able to spend any time in for the past six years."

So whatever way departure from the show affected her, it apparently wasn't going to be in the pocketbook.

On the monitor, the run-through progressed. Ms. Geller frowned. "I must say I don't see any point in making that change. Oh, well, it's not my worry."

The run-through ended. The hands of the clock stood at ten minutes to three. Josh had not reappeared.

At this rate, he was going to miss the

broadcast, but I didn't have much chance to think about it. The electricity in the air as the run-through ended was almost palpable through the monitor. It spread, like a building tidal wave. I eased myself out of the office, and the red-carpeted corridor was also alive. Everyone, needed there or not, was migrating inexorably in the direction of the sound stage.

For a few minutes, the heavy metal doors were open. Makeup people and hairdressers were rushing around. Two TV monitors had been hung, on long metal poles, from the high grid which sustained the hanging lights. I peered upwards, vaguely making out a catwalk even further up. The monitors were for the benefit of actors who, in position for the following scene, would not be able to see what was happening immediately before.

Aunt Jane touched my elbow. "Come with me up to the control room. You'll have to be deathly quiet."

"Wait!" I ran for my attache case and hurried after her. Behind us, the metal doors clanged shut. In the control room, Jake Fisk was counting off the time.

"Two minutes . . . one. . . ." He was speaking by microphone to Dan Wageman's headset. In front of the Judson Armitage living room, an assistant director raised an arm. Brought it down. The sound of *Lust for Life's* theme music flooded everywhere. We were on the air.

After that, everything moved like a flood that could not be dammed. From one scene to another, professionally, smoothly, so that if viewers had not heard the announcer's voice saying, "And now, *live*, we bring you . . ." they would have thought it was a show like any other.

The booth, I discovered, had monitors turned on the props dump area and on Aunt Jane's office. In the first, office personnel and the designers were watching avidly. In the executive office, selected media people were enthroned on the Chinese chairs.

The show built toward its climax. The final scene — in Celia's room — began. I reached into my attache case, took something out, leaned forward. Did a double take. That last scene I'd watched yesterday — the one in which Celia laughed in her lover's face — had been written into this earlier episode. The same things occurred: the love-hate tension, the threat of physical violence, the look on Celia's face.

The man stormed out. Celia laughed again. She did that half-touching, half-terrifying transition into puzzled child. Moved to the bureau, humming. She lifted the music box and for a heart-tugging moment stood looking with infinite sadness off into the future as her fingers gently stroked the carving.

As unobtrusively as possible, I stood up and moved to the glass viewing panel at the far end where I would not disturb anyone. I lifted my camera — and waited.

Celia's fingers pushed the lever. The music coiled. Then she lifted the lid.

Suddenly the set was filled with smoke. With smoke, and a clap of light, and the cameras panned the room crazily, and closed in at last on Celia, lying on the floor, her forehead wounded and covered with "blood," which a makeup woman had crawled, unseen through the smoke, to quickly add.

Even in the sealed-off control room, we could feel the waves of shock. My camera clicked swiftly, recording every reaction as cast and crew stood frozen, waiting for the off-the-air signal, before they exploded into speech.

Chapter 7

The red on-the-air light went out and everyone sprang to life.

Aunt Jane, with Mr. Doyle and me behind her, hurtled out of the control room and towards the sound stage. At the same moment, the metal doors burst open and everyone who had been watching the show on monitors surged in. *They* hadn't seen the makeup woman's crawl; they thought the joker had struck again — live, on camera.

"*Leslie — !*" "Good lord, is she dead?" The designers, and various cast members on hand but not part of today's broadcast, rushed for Leslie Swayne. Margaret Geller, white as a sheet, strode toward Aunt Jane. Behind her, Leslie pulled herself up.

"It's all right! Just Celia's swan song! This is what's known as going out with a bang."

There were more shocked exclamations — so the secret really had been kept, I thought

— then Leslie was engulfed in tears and hugs. Over it all, Margaret Geller's voice rang out.

"How dare you!" She was so angry she was shaking, but her voice rasped like a knife and carried to the far ends of the hall. "Celia's story has been carefully developed for a year, and it's integral to the plot! How *dare* you write a character out, and fire an actress I chose, without consulting me?"

"Margaret," Aunt Jane said gently, "come inside. It's not the time nor place —"

"It certainly is!" the writer snapped. "This was *my* territory fully fifteen years before you came. You wouldn't be here if I hadn't brought you! This is *my* show — I taught it to you — and if you think you can violate the basic concept —"

"But I can." Jane Palmer Kirby's words dropped like chips of ice into the sudden stillness. "I'm executive producer, and I make the ultimate decisions. Even the head writer cannot dictate those decisions, or countermand them. Especially after she's retired."

The tension building in the room peaked like a wave and burst.

For a moment, I thought Ms. Geller was going to strike Aunt Jane. Or have a heart attack, one or the other. She did neither; she turned on her heel and swept out of the sound stage like an exiled queen. The media people, scenting a story, split in three directions — Jane Palmer Kirby, Margaret Geller,

Leslie Swayne. Leslie, wiping off stage blood with a tissue someone had pressed into her hand, didn't even seem to see them.

"Margaret —" She hurried out after the older woman.

Those currents I'd felt yesterday were eddying everywhere. Where were Josh and his surveillance cameras, now that I needed them? The exhilaration of the live broadcast had been cut off by the shock of Celia's demise.

Jane Palmer Kirby found a patch of empty floor space with a light focused on it, and took center stage. "May I have your attention, please!"

The room hushed. Deliberately, she took a minute, turning her gaze one way and another. When she spoke, her voice was encouraging and calm. "Let me assure you, first of all, that at this moment we have no further elimination of characters planned. All of your contracts will be honored for their full term, and if any changes are contemplated you will be given the normal number of weeks' notice. I am sorry that Celia's murder had to be sprung on you just now, but the live broadcast was too valuable an opportunity to miss. An opinion with which, I'm relieved to be able to say, Leslie Swayne concurred. Only the pressures of events, yesterday and today, necessitated the rest of you being kept in the dark."

"What about Margaret Geller?" one of

the media people shouted. Only my knowing her so well told me Aunt Jane was taking a deep breath.

"Ms. Geller, after a long and distinguished career, has chosen to retire from *Lust for Life*. She plans some rest and travel, after which I'm sure. . . ."

Half of my mind was wishing Josh would get back here. The other half was watching as many *Lust for Life* faces as possible, wishing I could use my camera. My eyes swept around, from side to side, and overhead —

The TV monitor, on its pole a few feet above Aunt Jane's head, began to vibrate gently —

"Jane!" I screamed, and flung myself forward, knocking her to the ground. I hit the ground also, a half second later. And in a half second more, though it seemed like hours, something enormously sharp and heavy hit my left foot, and there was another puff of smoke.

Sparks shot, and glass rained everywhere. Josh, ashen-faced, barreled over from the door he had just entered, and knelt beside me.

"I'm all right —" I tried to move, but the remains of the TV monitor held me down. Josh, and the actor who played Judson Armitage, and one of Josh's technician buddies held me down.

"Don't move! Don't either of you women move until I get the power to that line turned off!" the head electrician roared, charging out.

"Ms. Kirby —" Thank heaven I'd remembered to say Ms. Kirby — but had I shouted *Jane* or *Aunt Jane* before? If I had, no one seemed to have noticed.

"She'll be all right," Mr. Doyle called. He had his arm around my aunt. I heard her own voice, carefully controlled, saying, "Don't anybody panic."

"Why shouldn't they panic?" Margaret Geller demanded from the far door. She looked — it sounds cruel to say it — like a bat out of hell. "Everyone knows there are malignant forces at work, and they're growing stronger. What will it take to make you people realize it? Someone getting killed?"

"That's enough," Mr. Doyle said sharply.

I heard my aunt murmur something in remonstrance. It was odd — I hadn't been hit on the head, yet everything was alternating in clarity and dark, like scenes in a strobe light. My leg was alternately numb and throbbing. My sight and hearing were alternately foggy and very sharp.

Josh crouched beside me and clasped both of my hands tightly. "The blasted traffic — I thought I'd get back here faster if I took a cab, but we got caught in the garment district."

Even in my pain and anxiety, my mind was able to be tickled that Josh the sophisticate was still too new to the East Coast to know his way around the city as well as I did. I half smiled, but Josh couldn't see the humor.

"I should have been here. If I hadn't cut out just because I was getting bored —"

"Josh, stop that! Even if you had been here, you couldn't have prevented it —" I stopped abruptly.

"What?"

"Not now."

Josh started to protest, saw my eyes, and got the point. Fortunately, no one else did. The technicians were clearing away the remains of the monitor, no longer electricity-charged. Somebody's hands explored me for broken bones. Somebody's arms lifted me onto a stretcher — how convenient, *Lust for Life* had an emergency room set, fully stocked with props — and bore me over to the nearest sofa. Aunt Jane was being treated in the same fashion. With one exception.

"I think she may have a broken leg," a woman said. I remembered vaguely that one of the regular cast members happened to be a registered nurse.

"An ambulance is on the way. And a doctor." That was Linda Partridge. The nurse, who turned out to be that lovely Caroline Armitage actress, knelt at my feet with a first-aid kit and cleaned my leg, which seemed to have a deep gash in it. She looked up and smiled.

"Don't worry. You'll be fine."

"Ms. Kirby —"

"She'll be fine, too. Thanks to your quick thinking, dear. You knocked her almost out of range, so only her leg was hit. It would have been worse, had the monitor landed directly on her head.

I shuddered.

Then Leslie Swayne was there, talking in low tones to Josh. Then the two plainclothes detectives who'd been staked out at the studio, in case the joker got cute, tried to throw both of them out and interview me. Josh tried to get masterful and was overruled. He did get to stay, after it was pointed out that he and I were jointly on the premises to investigate the joker, also.

I repeated what little I could remember — looking around, seeing the monitor start to shimmy, acting on instinct. "I didn't see anything else," I said for the fourth time.

The ambulance attendants and doctor arrived and pulled rank on the detectives. Then the medical people and I had a fight, which turned into a fight between Josh and me, over whether I had to go to the hospital.

"Shut up and go!" Aunt Jane said strongly, overhearing. "It's necessary for the sake of our insurance!" We got to ride together in the ambulance, which was more than Josh did. He and Mr. Doyle followed in what must have been one hell of a taxi ride.

There were attendants and a detective in

the ambulance, so my aunt and I couldn't talk. She was flat on a stretcher — at least they let me sit up — but I saw her hand reach out. I took it and held it tight.

"Do what you're told to," Aunt Jane said. Her voice was weak, but her intention strong. "I'll be in touch, as soon as I can."

When we reached the emergency room, activity proceeded the way I'd seen in a hundred TV shows, not to mention in Dad's hospital. I was cleaned up, sewn up, and parked at last in a wheelchair. Nobody would tell me a thing about Aunt Jane. At last they let Josh near me.

"I called your dad," he said. "He's ordered a private ambulance to come take you home. Take *us* home."

"Don't you think it's more important for you to —"

"No."

I didn't feel up to fighting, and to tell the truth I didn't want to. I snuggled next to Josh in the ambulance, very grateful for his arm around me during a surprisingly painful ride. The highway was a mass of potholes, and my leg was throbbing.

The ambulance drew up with a flourish before my house, and it was a toss-up as to who got there first — my parents, or Cordelia and the hackers, all agog.

"Please, will everybody just buzz off?" I said impolitely. "Except Josh. I've got to talk to Josh."

"Not until you've talked to me first," my father retorted firmly. He superintended my transportation to my bedroom and gave my leg another thorough going-over.

"You'll live," he said at last.

I was getting tired of hearing that everything would be all right. "What about Aunt Jane?" I demanded.

"She'll live, too. I talked to the doctor who took care of her. Her leg's not broken, only badly bruised. There are bones broken in her foot. At that point, they were still up in the air about putting on a cast. But your aunt had made it very clear she was going to sleep in her own bed tonight." Dad grinned. "Jane's not a redhead for nothing."

"I want to see Josh."

"I know, sweetie. And Cordelia's raising Cain to see you, too."

"Not Cordelia, not until tomorrow. Just Josh." I was surprised to discover I was very tired.

So Josh came in, and I told him as much as I could remember of what had happened at the studio while he wasn't there. Josh was on a guilt trip about that. While I had to admit I could have used him, it was silly of him to think he could have prevented the accident, and I said so.

"We don't even know it *wasn't* an accident!"

"Don't we?" Josh asked starkly.

"I didn't see anything that could prove it.

Look, can't we talk about the rest of this tomorrow?"

"I'm sorry," Josh said.

"I am, too," I said quietly. "This has been a grueling day for both of us." I held my arms out and Josh bent down. We hugged for a long time and I believed that everything would be all right.

Josh stood up when we heard a knock on the door. Mother came in, bringing a dinner tray. He bent down again to kiss me goodnight, and left.

"You won't have to stay in bed," Mother said. "Your father says you won't even need crutches or a wheelchair, but I guess I'm entitled to spoil you for tonight." She snapped on the TV and we watched the news coverage of the live broadcast and its dangerous aftermath. The network — Aunt Jane's network — was playing it up to the hilt, which would be good for *Lust for Life*. Fortunately they hadn't found out about the joker.

Mother had gone, and I was drowsing off to sleep, when the telephone rang. I reached for it groggily.

It wasn't Aunt Jane. A slightly familiar voice said, "This is Leslie Swayne. May I speak to Sidney Scott Webster?"

I pushed myself up, suddenly wide awake. "This is she."

"I hope it's all right, my calling. Jane Kirby suggested it. Actually, she gave me your number."

"How is she?" I demanded. I heard Leslie chuckle.

"In bed with a splitting headache, a few cracked bones, and a case of absolute fury. How are *you?* And do you want us to get together some time tomorrow?"

I didn't make a sound, but she must have known I was surprised. She went on, in a slightly altered tone, "Didn't Jane Kirby tell you? At least for the next three months, I'm going to be the *Lust for Life* head writer."

Chapter 8

Early next morning a council converged in the war room — not as early as I'd wanted, because Dad and Mother put all four feet down. All the same, Josh arrived with the breakfast coffee. He looked as though he'd slept in his clothes — Josh, the debonair!

"Did you sleep in them, or just throw them in the corner?" I inquired with interest.

"Now that you mention it, I don't think I did sleep. And if you can wisecrack, you must be feeling better." Josh spread out yards of computer paper. "I fed everything we know so far about The Joker into the database." So our weirdo had officially acquired a name now, I thought. "Read it over and see if I've left anything out. Then maybe we can psych out a pattern somewhere."

"I can give you a pattern. Steadily accelerating destructive behavior, starting with minor pranks and spreading."

"To what? To whom? And why?" Josh

frowned. "If we could pin that down, we'd have more chance of getting a handle on it."

"Wanting to slow down the show. And/or stop the show. And/or he's simply psycho, as has been suggested."

"There's nothing simple about the situation," Josh said forcefully. "And regardless of how the tricks started out, yesterday was different."

I frowned, then nodded. "Somebody could have gotten killed. *Aunt Jane* could have gotten killed. You think it was a deliberate attempt at murder?"

"I can tell you one thing," Josh answered. "The monitor fell because the clamp that held it in place had been almost totally unscrewed. Mr. Doyle told me in the taxi cab. He said the head electrician was up on the grid, just before Celia's last scene began, and he automatically checked all the clamps as he walked past them. Whoever loosened that did it during the last four minutes of the broadcast, or in the first ten minutes after it was over."

We looked at each other.

"There's something else you haven't heard," I said. I told him about Leslie's telephone call. Josh's eyebrows went up.

"Your aunt hired her as the new writer?"

"It makes sense. She used to be a writer. She certainly knows the show well enough to be able to pick up the threads. And she knows how to handle action and dialogue. A lot of TV actors write, you know."

"If your aunt *did* hire her."

"How else would Leslie have gotten this phone number? I know, I know!" I waved away Josh's tolerant expression. "I'm going to phone Aunt Jane, anyway. That's why I told Leslie not to come out here until this afternoon."

"Aren't you the least bit skeptical about Leslie Swayne's innocence?"

"Honestly, I'm not. I can't prove why, it's just —"

"I know, you 'have a feeling!' "

"Don't knock it 'til you've tried it," I said tartly. "Anyway, Leslie was on stage the whole time during that last scene."

"How about the ten minutes before the TV crashed?"

The picture of Leslie rushing out after Margaret flooded back to me. "I would like to know," I admitted reluctantly, "why Leslie had been so — calm, about Celia being bumped. If it was my job being axed, I wouldn't be."

I didn't know how early it would be safe to call Aunt Jane, but she beat me to it, ringing just as Josh and I finished breakfast. She confirmed everything Leslie Swayne had said.

"She's written before. So when I had to tell her Celia was being written out at once, I brought it up. And she agreed."

"Aunt Jane? When did you have that talk with Leslie?"

"As soon as I got back to the studio, after phoning you Thursday morning."

So Leslie Swayne had known she was off the cast, when she'd sat there in the coffee-colored slip, looking so very calm.

I was just off the phone when Cordelia, Steve, and Ceegee arrived. We convened in my office — I had the couch to myself, by virtue of my wounded state — and Cordelia produced a notebook. "Listen up, children. I am about to educate you on the highlights of *Lust for Life*'s twenty lusty years." While I had been at the studio being heroic, Cordelia had been cutting school to hole up with the master plot book.

Josh, Steve, and Ceegee arranged themselves to listen, and Cordelia shot me an impish glance. It wasn't often she got to expound and have those three attentive. "OK, the core of *Lust for Life*, or any soap opera, for that matter, is relationships. It doesn't matter whether the stories are true to life, or kind of adult fantasies, or mysteries, or action. What people tune in on, what they get hooked on, is the characters and how they feel about each other."

There were ribald under-breath comments from Steve and Ceegee, which she ignored superbly. "Most soaps revolve around two main families. Usually one upper-crust establishment, the other down-to-earth. They don't have to be real blood-related families. In *General Hospital*, the 'family' is the hospital staff. In *Lust for Life*, the Armitages are upper-crust. The 'just-folks' used to be the Kinkaids, only most of them have been canned over the years. Now there's just Dr. Olivia Kinkaid Armitage and her daughter Nell.

"Nell's father was a crusading newspaper editor. He died. It's never been explained quite how. Olivia married Judson Armitage, who's Josh thirty years from now, if you know what I mean. Rich, powerful, and knows it."

Josh looked indignant. Cordelia gave him an angelic smile. "Anyway, Nell's furious about the marriage, at her stepfather, and especially at her new stepbrother, Greg Armitage. He's Joe College — moody, gorgeous. He and Nell are the new young lust interest. They throw in a teenage sex story every summer," she added, parenthetically, "to get kids to watch. The Greg/Nell bit started last July. It hasn't gotten far, but not for Greg's lack of trying. Nell's the 'nice girl.' The 'bad girl' is Emmy Polnitski, who's after Greg or anything else in trousers. I'll get to her later."

By this time Steve and Ceegee, who had started out prepared to be bored, were perking up with interest. Josh was fascinated. "How do they ever keep all the plot lines straight?" he marveled.

"Just the way a conductor keeps all the different melodies in an orchestra score straight," Cordelia said blandly, and made a gesture of chalking up a score. Josh is a fiend for classical music. "Actually," she said, relenting, "it's not as hard as you would think. You usually have the same basic characters — hero, loyal friend, long-suffering heroine, witch, sympathetic neurotics, *un*-sympathetic neurotics, driven-by-success, on-way-up-in-world, on-way-down — on three different age levels. There are characters in their sixties or older, that once were the main focus of the stories but now are the supportive grandparents. Then there are the 35-to-55-year-olds, still sexy and gorgeous. And there are the young adults, some still in school, some starting their careers."

"You mean they're interchangeable parts in the scripts?" Steve asked. "That's crazy!"

"I know it. But it used to work. It still does, where the relationship problems are concerned. My gosh, you've seen my parents going at it," Cordelia said inelegantly. "They're in their forties, but their romance sure hasn't cooled! It's when the writers use the same action and dialogue for the young characters that the scenes don't work. Or when you get the feeling they've resurrected the young love scenes from ten years ago." Cordelia turned to me. "I've had that feeling with *Lust for Life* a lot."

I nodded. I could see exactly what she meant.

"What about themes?" Josh asked. He'd been keying into his computer rapidly as she spoke.

"All the classics. Love and hate. Life and death. Good and evil. The seven deadly sins. Sex and the lack of it. Mistaken identity. Crime — its discovery and its concealment. In the end, justice always triumphs and virtue always pays. And nobody ever stays happy or untroubled for more than a few months, or everything would get awfully boring."

She zipped through the other main story characteristics. Main characters in professions that bring them into contact with lots of people — medicine, law, big business, politics. Settings in which a lot of paths can cross — hospitals, lawyers' or district attorneys' offices, restaurants, newspaper offices, hotels. "In *Lust for Life* you have all of the above. Plus The Pub, which is owned by mystery man Dan Rawlins, who's really the illegitimate son of tycoon Giles Stratton Tolen, who's been married to Giles Tolen's ex-wife, and a lot of other women besides. And oh, yes, it's the thing now to always have a few minority-group characters, and some blue-collars. Otherwise known as hitting all the audience bases."

Ceegee groaned. "Just think of it in terms of what it's like in our school," Cordelia told him sweetly, "and you'll get the picture."

"I get it. I'm just overwhelmed. But I can see how you can get hooked, because nothing ever has a beginning or an end, does it?"

"Never. Characters even rise again from the dead," Cordelia said serenely.

"Maybe we can find some to resurrect in *Lust for Life*," I said. "That could be almost as enthralling as a murder."

"I've made a list of possibilities," Cordelia said demurely. The boys were looking at her with respect, and I congratulated myself on having brought her in on this. Come to think of it, Leslie Swayne reminded me of Cordelia — and so had the character Celia, back in her sympathetic, unpsycho days.

When Cordelia's soap seminar was done, we got down to business at our various computers. I debated on communicating with Samantha via Alpha, but settled for a keyboard on my lap. Josh got the guys started entering Cordelia's data into databases — Steve working with plots, and Ceegee with character relationships — and Cordelia started plowing through the summaries of other soaps that Josh had obtained from the lady at the magazine.

"I'm making a list of good plots I've run across in romance novels lately," she said. Ceegee laughed.

"What about some of the ones going on around our school?"

"You have a point. At least they'd be true

to today's young adults. I use the word 'adult' loosely. Could we base a story on you?" Cordelia asked him sweetly.

My mother, bless her, provided lunch for all. At two-thirty a car pulled into the driveway, and it was Leslie Swayne. She looked much like the old Celia used to, in a silk shirt and slim slacks, with no makeup and a scarf around her hair. She and I withdrew into my bedroom for a conference.

"Jane told me you already have the master plot book. I've brought the scripts for all the shows that are already taped." Leslie hesitated. "Do you suppose I could use one of those computers? I could key in script changes as we discuss them."

"All the ones we have here are in use." I didn't want to part with Samantha. "But I'm sure Ceegee would bring over another one." I hollered, and Ceegee went next door and obliged.

"I went through most of these scripts last night," Leslie said, "and made a list of changes that would be simple. How soon do you think you'll have data on what's most successful?"

"The crew's working on that in the war room right now."

"Oh, good." Leslie settled herself in my big chair, her feet tucked up under her, looking like a very little girl behind the big-rimmed glasses she popped on absently as she read.

"Can I ask you something?" I said abruptly.

She looked up, sobering as she caught my tone. "Of course."

"You're not the least bit upset about Celia being axed, are you? Why?"

She didn't answer at first. Then a small smile curved her lips. "You might as well know. We'd planned to keep it a secret a bit longer, but I've told Jane, anyway. I'm pregnant. The doctor only confirmed it Wednesday night."

The night before I'd seen her as an island of enigmatic calm in a sea of tension.

"I've had two miscarriages already, so this time my doctor laid down the law. I came in Thursday intending to tell Jane I couldn't play Celia any longer, when she beat me to the punch. So you can see," she finished, "why I wasn't devastated by the news. And it was getting difficult living with Celia, anyway. But writing — that's different." She glanced at me, reclining on my back with Samantha's no-cord-needed keyboard propped against my legs, and smiled. "Writing I can do at home. *And* while resting!"

"Leslie? What do you think is behind The Joker?"

Leslie's smile vanished. "I don't know."

"But you have an idea, don't you?" I sat up, heedless of the throbbing in my leg at the sudden movement. "Please tell me."

"I'm not sure," Leslie said carefully. She

turned and looked out the window at the burgeoning trees. "You've felt it, haven't you?" she said at last. "The tension?"

"Yes. I wondered if it was because of the — tricks. Or the ratings troubles."

Leslie shook her head. "It started after the ratings slipped, and long before the tricks. The first week of July, last summer, when Jane Kirby started altering the tone of the show. I know people will tell you it was later, but it was then. I noticed before they did. I pick up on things like that," she said simply.

I nodded.

"It got worse after the first few weeks. As though something was fighting against the changes."

"Was there fighting?" I asked, and Leslie said, grimly. "Oh, yes." "You get comfortable with things the way they are. Especially if you think your job might be at stake."

I rapidly ran my mind back over the actors I knew of who had been on for years. "You mean you think The Joker's one of the Old Guard?"

"I didn't say that," Leslie replied instantly. "I said the tension could have begun with them. Once it begins, it spreads. And it's particularly hard for someone with a distinguished career to be in that kind of position. To be out-of-date, no longer needed. It's world-destroying."

A vivid picture rose before my eyes. "Like Margaret Geller?" I asked quietly.

Leslie wouldn't look at me. "I'm worried about Margaret," she said compassionately. "Her whole life, her whole career, have been wrapped up in *Lust for Life* for so long. She created other shows, too, but this is the one most identified with her. And she's been so engrossed in the Celia story. Almost as if she was identifying with it." She stopped abruptly.

I waited.

"Margaret brought me into the show, you know," Leslie said. "She wrote the role for me. I didn't know in the beginning that Celia would end up — possessed. Maybe she didn't know it herself. But the character's been Margaret's pride and joy. I was her protegee. She thought of Jane Kirby as her protegee. It was hard on her, when we both started insisting the Celia story line had gone sour."

"Let me get this straight," I said at last, carefully. "Do you think, do you even *begin* to think, that Margaret Geller could be behind the tricks?"

Leslie didn't answer directly. She said instead, "You do know, don't you, that Margaret Geller used to own the show? She sold it to the sponsor, for a fabulous figure, a few years before Jane Palmer Kirby came aboard. But she still always felt she owned it. She still ran the show. Everyone let her — because she projected so much power. Because she knew the show better than anyone. Because they were afraid of what she could do to them if she got angry. But mostly because she was the absolute best at what she did. Until this year. This year it's been Jane Palmer Kirby who knows best and has the power."

Chapter 9

For a minute, I just stared. Then I said, "Hang on. Josh had better hear about this."

"You stay off your leg. I'll get him," Leslie said, and did.

I told him about the power struggle and about Margaret Geller's owning *Lust for Life* up until a while ago. Josh's immediate reaction was, "Why didn't I know about this before?"

"Most people do. Jane Kirby probably thought you knew, or she may not have considered it important. Margaret Geller sold her rights to *Lust for Life* long before Jane came on to it, after all."

Or maybe this was one of the things Aunt Jane was holding back, because she didn't want to prejudice us. I made a note to have a little talk with her about that.

"*I* should have known," Josh said frankly. "I always keep up with business news. I must have overlooked this because I thought daytime TV was trivial, and that was stupid."

Or because he would have been — what? All of ten years old when Geller sold the show? I didn't embarrass him by pointing that out. Come to think of it, Josh at ten was probably already hooked on *The Wall Street Journal*. And I was already watching *Lust for Life*. I racked my brains to remember what it was like back then.

Come to think of it, not so different from now. People got undressed more now, and talked about some things more frankly. Actors had gotten older. Other than that, it sounded and looked the same. That was Aunt Jane's problem in a nutshell, wasn't it?

"Tell us more about Margaret Geller," I said.

Leslie spread her hands. "That's hard. I never realized 'til just now that none of us know much about her outside the show. I don't know if she *has* a life outside the show. She had a husband once, but whether he's dead or they're divorced, I have no idea. It was long ago. I know she had a daughter, and they didn't get along. The girl was wild. I think she did drugs in the sixties and had to be institutionalized."

"What became of her?" Josh asked alertly.

"She died of a drug overdose many years ago. That I *do* know. Margaret was doing some writing for another soap that I was in at the time, and we sent flowers. I know she went through a bad time then. I remember finding her in the film lab, crying, and then sitting talking to her for a long time. I hadn't thought the Dragon Lady knew how to cry. That's what she's known as in the business, you know. The Dragon Lady."

"Is that how you two got to know each other? The daughter's death?"

"We didn't get to know — Oh, you mean the bit about her writing the role of Celia for me, and thinking of me as a protegee? That wasn't unusual. The soap opera world's a small one, you know. There's a solid core of performers who make their whole careers in it. They go from show to show. Producers and directors and writers know their work, and know they're dependable. Ross Taylor, who plays Judson Armitage, started as a child actor, and he was a romantic lead in another soap for years." She named the show. "Five weeks after his character died in a plane crash, he took over the Judson role in *Lust*. Rumor has it that other character's about to miraculously reappear, and the producers want to lure him back for it. So far he's not lureable, but with the fate of our show so equivocal, who knows?"

"How did you find out about that?"

Leslie flashed a gamine grin. "Easy. Marian Clark, who plays Judith Armitage, Judson's current sister-in-law, is married to an actor on the other show. I told you it's a small world."

And clearly one we needed to know more

about. I reached for Samantha's keyboard and started feeding her information as Josh pumped Leslie further. By the time we finished, we had a fat file of substantiatable and unsubstantiatable gossip, and at least four people who had good reason to want *Lust for Life*, or Jane Palmer Kirby, slowed down or stopped.

And the natives in the war room were getting restless. I heard Ceegee plaintively demanding sustenance, and I shouted that he could raid the refrigerator if he used discretion. Steve and he went to do so, with Cordelia along to provide the discretion, and Josh went down to make a pot of coffee. Everything and everybody, my mother and dad included, ended up back in my bedroom. By now, my gentleman hackers were freaking out from an overdose of soap plots, and the fact that Leslie worked in the industry did nothing to cramp their style.

"You're the one who's been playing that weirdo Sidney talked about? How do you come up with that stuff? And how do you stand it?"

"I researched it with a psychiatrist friend, and visited some clinics and halfway houses. And remember, Celia didn't *know* she was going mad — or becoming possessed; I wasn't told which it would turn out to be. She thought *she* was sane, and the rest of the world was weird." Leslie's eyes had a wicked glint. "Haven't you ever had that feeling?

And don't you get your kicks out of whatever programming's most difficult, whether or not the objective of the program's a concern of yours?"

"Score one for Ms. Swayne," Dad said solemnly, extending his hand.

"You're at Lakeland Hospital, aren't you? My physician's thinking of consulting you, if I run into any difficulties." It turned out Leslie lived a half-hour's ride away, closer to the George Washington Bridge. All this led naturally into the news of her pregnancy, and I breathed a sigh of relief. Dad knew her doctor; Dad could check whether the reasons she gave for not caring about Celia's being terminated were true.

Leslie also offered the loan of VCR tapes of a year's worth of *Lust for Life.* "I set my machine to tape the show every day, so I can study it that night."

That was all the invitation the hackers needed to be appallingly gracious about pointing out the show's flaws. It wouldn't have been so bad, I thought, outraged, if they'd at least watched the show several times. Their wisdom was based on watching yesterday while cutting class, and saturation in the data Cordelia had provided. Leslie didn't seem to mind.

"So you think the younger characters aren't true to life?" she asked innocently. "What *should* their stories be?"

Within half an hour she had drawn out of

them a list of every famous and infamous thing to happen in our school — no, our whole town! — in the past year. After five minutes I'd caught on to what she was up to, and started keyboarding Samantha. Leslie caught me at it, and winked.

"I think we have enough for two years' worth of plot lines now," she said at last. "Don't you hackers have some data to crunch somewhere? I'll keep Cordelia here, if you don't mind."

They didn't mind. Cordelia was enchanted, and Leslie clearly was impressed with Cordelia's understanding of the ins and outs of soap opera programming. The three of us spent an intensive hour and a half on the scripts for Monday through Wednesday's shows. It was possible, by cutting out bits of dialogue here and there, and splicing in scenes from later shows, to eliminate Celia or references to her entirely and still have all but three to five minutes' worth of the tape needed for each day.

"I'll start writing that now. That is — good grief!" Leslie had looked at her watch. "It's six-thirty. My husband will be frantic." We'd gotten so slaphappy with work, weariness, and job satisfaction that we'd forgotten about the time.

"Do you want to call him?"

"I think I'd better." Leslie reached for the phone. I hesitated, but Cordelia the confident volunteered what I'd been thinking.

"Why don't you tell him to come on over? You don't live far, and I just know Mrs. Webster's downstairs producing enough food for an army."

In the end, that's exactly what happened; everybody stayed, including Josh's mother whom my mother thought to call and ask, and Leslie and her husband. Bill Swayne proved to be a big, easygoing man and he and my father instantly discovered a mutual scientific camaraderie. We all had, in fact, a very good time, and the subject of stolen tapes, strangled rats, and possible murder attempts were never mentioned. But the awareness of them was never far away. I saw it in my mother's eyes, my father's, Josh's. And especially in the Swaynes'.

It was not until Cordelia and the boys, including Josh, had left that anyone brought it up, and the person who did was Mr. Swayne.

He turned to my father. "I understand you have the rat someone planted for my wife to find."

Dad didn't beat about the bush. "I had it autopsied in my research lab. Not just I, but our best animal pathologist, looked at it. This morning I had our county coroner check the slides. It *was* strangled manually. I'm going to turn my data over to the New York police."

Chapter 10

Talking of split personalities, Sunday had one in spades, and so at that point did I. Maybe it was because my leg was stiff, and hurt, and Dad insisted on a certain amount of medication. Maybe *Lust for Life* — everything about *Lust for Life* — was getting to me. I woke up Sunday morning fantasizing fabulous plot lines for the show; I'm not proud of that, but it's true. Then the realization of all those other things came flooding back, and with them an awareness that a clock was ticking.

I dragged myself downstairs for breakfast and reached for the orange juice with one hand and the telephone with the other. Mother intercepted me.

"Not yet. Yes, I know you want to call Josh, but first your father and I have to talk to you."

Whenever she said "your father and I" . . .

I sat down and went rigid. "Nothing's happened to Aunt Jane, has it? Have you talked to her? You're *not* going to tell me to stop working on this!"

"No. Yes. I don't know. In that order." Mother gave Dad the look that meant, *Over to you.* Dad cleared his throat.

"Your aunt's at home. In a lot of pain, without a bodyguard, refusing to do anything about either and determined to go to work tomorrow. *I'm* determined to see her first. Which is why we had to get to you before you called in the hackers. Your mother and I are driving in, and you'd better come. As for you and *Lust for Life*, we'll go into that later, after I see Jane."

I phoned Josh and told him what was going on. He agreed with my father. I counted to ten. "I don't know how we're going to be able to work together, if you're planning to be the chauvinistic male —"

"Chauvinism be hanged. I don't want TV sets dropping on *me*, either," Josh said reasonably. "And I definitely think bodyguards are called for. You might try pointing out to Ms. Kirby that the New York Police Department is understaffed, and if people persist in putting themselves in dangerous positions they can't count on them being around to assure their safety."

He promised to call the rest of the work crew for me, and talked Mother into letting them work in my office in our absence, which was a big concession. My parents aren't thrilled at having people in the house when we're not home.

We found Aunt Jane on her bed in a Chinese robe, looking drawn and white. The purple shadows under her eyes stood out starkly. She had scripts, a dictating machine, a tape recorder, and a telephone all spread out around her. Dad took one look and raised an eyebrow, á la Josh.

"As your physician, I recommend a complete reversal of this treatment."

"You're not my physician, you're my brother-in-law. *My* physician, I think, isn't speaking to me. And don't bother telling me what I should or should not be doing. I know all that, and I can't help it. Not unless I want a permanent vacation."

"Do you really think that would happen if you took a few days off?" Mother asked in consternation.

"I can't afford to find out," Aunt Jane said grimly.

It opened up another avenue of thought. Someone trying to get Aunt Jane's job — could that be what was behind all this?

"The sponsors are more likely to take the show off the air completely," was Aunt Jane's opinion.

"What would happen then?"

"Another game show. At least for the time being. Then the sponsor might come up with a new soap. Jack Doyle hinted as much."

Another possibility. Who could think they'd benefit by the creation of a new show? Who could think they had so much clout and such a good track record that they could save a show when Jane Palmer Kirby could not? The name of Margaret Geller kept presenting itself.

I told Aunt Jane all Leslie had told me yesterday, and she nodded. "I've been worried about Margaret for some time. I said she's become . . . obsessed with her creations, with her 'people,' the characters and the flesh-and-blood. That's how she thought of all of us, as hers. It's sad. She wanted to be the Earth Mother of us all. But the harder she pushed, the harder people ran. . . . But drop a TV on us? I don't believe it."

Mother, I saw, could. Mother frowned. "I've known women like that in my hospital volunteer work. The Queen Bee syndrome."

"This one's called the Dragon Lady," I contributed. I saw Aunt Jane's flicker of surprise. "Didn't you know?"

"I'm beginning to think there are a lot of things I don't know. Of course, I'm at a disadvantage. I came onto the show at the top — executive producer. The person at the top never gets to tune in on the grapevine."

"Particularly when some very compassionate person is protecting her from the people under her, and protecting the people under her from her," Mother said surprisingly. We gaped at her. "A classic neurotic role — the indispensable, saintly crying-towel and fix-it, who little by little alienates everyone from each other, and winds up turning them against herself. We had them at the university when I taught math there, and we have them in professional and charitable organizations. They're the kiss of death."

I saw Dad nod. Aunt Jane managed a weak smile.

"We have them on the soaps, too. They start out as long-suffering heroines, and eventually become bores or else turn deadly, as you just described. As witness Celia."

"As witness Margaret Geller?"

"I just don't know."

"Jane," Dad said. "it's time to stop holding back. You have to turn whatever you know over to the police. Facts *and* suspicions."

"And you have to turn them over to Josh and me," I added. "I don't care if you want us to come into this with open minds. There isn't time for that any more."

When she didn't answer, I gave her a terse summary of the people Josh and I had concluded had means and motives, based on the gossip Leslie had shared with us. Margaret Geller wanting to stay in control of the show, possibly by becoming executive producer; wanting to protect her creation from Jane's changes. Ross Taylor, who played Judson Armitage, having a chance to resurrect his character on a higher rated show. An actor who'd been fired six months ago for consistently showing up stoned, who hadn't been able to get a job since. Leslie herself, who'd said she had trouble snapping out of the character of Celia. And three or four of the no-longer-quite-so-young performers, for whom major story alterations might mean curtains. They played the familiar main characters on whose strength the show would rest if it ran into temporary trouble — if, for example, tapes disappeared, or an executive producer was unavailable. Everyone had been *so* shocked when Aunt Jane had performed major surgery overnight, writing out Celia the day the show played live. . . .

Aunt Jane's eyes darkened. "I'm aware of most of that," she murmured. "That sort of thing goes on in any work situation. There are times I could cheerfully kill somebody. But we don't go around acting on our impulses."

"Somebody does," Dad said quietly.

I knew something else, too. Aunt Jane was lying. She hadn't known about all those things I said, and she wasn't taking them lightly. Not all of them. Something had given her a shock.

None of this went as orderly and cohesively as this sounds. There were constant interruptions. The phone rang, and it was Richard Conlon, the set designer. "We're scrapping all the Armitage living rooms," Aunt Jane told me with her hand across the mouthpiece. "And the Brannigan sets, and maybe we'll have the newspaper office go electronic. Richard's going to start redecorating the Judson Armitage house tomorrow. Yes, Richard? Fabric samples?"

The phone rang again, and it was Linda, saying she'd called in extra typists and the typing of revised scripts could begin at five a.m. The phone rang again, and it was the director of tomorrow's episode, wanting to know what surprises were in store. She told him. She hung up and, still arguing with us that means and motive did not equal criminal action, picked up the receiver and started to punch a number.

Dad went over to the wall and disconnected the line. "I can't stop you from talking, but I can stop you from being connected up with anyone on the other end. Jane, you have got to get some rest if you don't want to keel over, or wind up psycho yourself."

"I have a hired car and a wheelchair coming for me in the morning," Aunt Jane said distinctly. "I have my cleaning woman coming in early to help me dress. She will see that I eat my eggs and drink my milk like a good little girl. I have sixty-some-odd people at the studio who will run my errands and make my calls and do anything I need done, but I have to be there. I have to run the show. And *I* don't like Earth Mothers, male or female, trying to protect me from myself, any more than anyone else does!"

In the silence which greeted that announcement, we heard a key turn in the lock.

I was directly in line with the doors of Aunt Jane's apartment, so I could see. The door to her living room opened, and Margaret Geller came in. I saw her, reflected in the mirror over Aunt Jane's white couch. She came across to the bedroom doorway, and stopped, startled.

"Oh — I didn't know anyone would be here —"

Aunt Jane propped herself up on her elbows. "Margaret, what on earth are you doing here?"

"I was worried about your having no one to look after you. So, of course — Oh!" Her face cleared; softened. "Jane, you didn't think because of *yesterday* — *!* I was . . . stunned. I lashed out before I thought. You were right, of course, I don't own the show any more. But *Lust for Life* made me a very wealthy woman, and I'm tired of working, so why should I care? You certainly didn't think I'd let professional differences stand in the way of helping you when I was needed?"

In the awkward pause it was my mother's voice which came in, very clear and calm. "But she doesn't need it."

For the first time, Ms. Geller really looked at us. At Dad, enigmatic against the bookcase; Mother, standing her ground; me. "Oh, yes, you're . . ." She couldn't think of my name, and I did not supply it. She shrugged.

"Since I'm not needed, I might as well go."

"Just a minute," Aunt Jane said. "How did you get in here?"

The writer looked surprised. "Dear, don't you remember? You gave me a key last year, so I could come in and wait that night we were having a story conference and you were flying back in from out of town." She started for the door.

"Web," said my aunt, and Dad moved after her. Ms. Geller got to the outside door first, and opened it, and that's when things started getting larger than life.

A voice, stage-trained but not worried about its effect at the moment, shouted, "What the hell are you doing here? *Jane!*" Margaret Geller was propelled back toward the bedroom by Ross Taylor, who towered over her. He kicked the outside door shut behind him. "Why did you let her in here? Why the hell have you let any of these people in here? I told you I'd be over, and I told you not to let anybody in! If you don't have the sense to realize someone may be after you, woman —"

"And I told you not to come," Aunt Jane retorted. "For that matter, how do I know you're not The Joker? You didn't tell me Jay Gruen was trying to get you back on your old show!"

"I didn't tell you because I didn't want you upset. Or jumping to conclusions," Ross said roughly. "And if you can seriously contemplate for one minute that I want to harm you —"

"Incidentally, I did not let Ms. Geller in. She had a key. Take it away from her, will you, and then walk her to the door." Aunt Jane's spirit wasn't failing, but her strength was. My parents looked at each other. Ross Taylor peremptorily took Ms. Geller's handbag, found and confiscated the key, and marched her out of the apartment. He closed and dead-bolted the door after her.

"I've told you to keep that dead-bolt on," he told my aunt, dangerously mild.

"I think," my mother said distinctly, "it's time for us to leave." She marched to the door with my father, who looked stunned. I trailed after them very thoughtfully. My mother was the only one who looked particularly relieved as we rode down in the elevator.

"Well," she said cryptically. "Jane and Ross Taylor. Who would have thought?"

Chapter 11

"Okay," Josh said, locking his arms behind his head, "what do we have so far?"

It was late Sunday. Josh and Samantha and I were in conference in what Cordelia now referred to as "the boss's private office," namely my bedroom. Beyond the door, market research was still in progress in the war room. The three of us were concentrating on criminal research.

"What we have is a bunch of people with motives. And a choice of objectives. To get *Lust for Life* off the air. To just slow it down. To make themselves indispensable to its staying *on* the air. To eliminate Jane Palmer Kirby — temporarily or permanently — for any or all of the above reasons, or for just sheer spite. I don't *think* anyone has any other reasons for attacking her," I added thoughtfully.

"In other words, there's a lot you really don't know about your aunt's life," Josh said bluntly. Remembering the incident with Ross Taylor, I had to agree.

I filled Josh in on that, and my mother's interpretation, and Josh snorted. "All we need now is romantic complications."

"Relationships between people are a dynamic in any situation. Don't rule them out."

"Now you're starting to sound like Cordelia. I wasn't ruling them out. I was just groaning about one more variable to have to factor in."

"Now *you're* sounding like a statistician."

"Thanks for the compliment." Josh rose. "I have a program at home for calculating probabilities. Be right back."

He returned with an assortment of program disks and his little black book. "Shove over," he commanded. "If I use Samantha I'll get answers faster."

"What answers? And from where?"

"You don't want to know," Josh said absently. "Just hand me the suspect list. In fact, you'd better give me the entire list of *Lust for Life* personnel."

Josh had access, authorized or otherwise, to a number of data banks via modem and the numbers in that black book of his. By his code of ethics, he was not a hacker, but by his code of ethics the ends could often justify the means. I had a feeling it would be better if I didn't know whether this was one of those times.

One of Samantha's expensive assets is

that she's amenable to any computer language and compatible with any operating system. Josh booted her up with his program disks. Samantha and he had a battle of wills for a few minutes, then she started humming merrily along.

"Margaret Geller sure doesn't need to work any longer," Josh said soon thereafter. "Boy, I wish I had her stock portfolio! And she does own a house in the south of France, also a couple of condos that she rents out, plus being a partner in some industrial real estate deals. That lady's smart."

"How did you find all that out?" I demanded.

"Don't ask. No major debts. No close relations living."

"Ask about the husband," I said, forgetting about my scruples.

"Name: George Albert Geller. Civil Engineer, former professor. Divorced from Margaret in 1959. Whereabouts in recent years unknown."

It did seem unlikely that this late in the game he'd decide to attack *Lust for Life* when Margaret Geller no longer even owned it. Josh went on working his way down the list of names. He discovered that two of the backstage crew played the horses; there were three people with known alcohol problems; and three who'd been charged with possession, two of marijuana and one of cocaine. "I don't like this," I said uneasily.

"You'd like it a darn sight less if The Joker's acting out some drug fantasy, and nobody knows it," Josh said grimly, and went on with his fishing expedition. At last he made a printout and switched program disks. "Don't worry," he said. "I didn't turn up anything really bad. No psychos or axe murderers or racketeers."

"What are we going to do with that, now that we have it?"

"*We* don't have it; I do. You didn't want to be involved, remember? And I'm not going to do anything with the information unless I have to, other than use it to figure probabilities. I'm not a gutter journalist," Josh said. He sounded tired. "But if the police are building a case and I have evidence, then I won't be able to withhold it. Don't worry. I won't bring your name into it."

"Don't be silly!" I said strongly. "I signed the contract for this job, and we're in it together. . . . What are you going to do about probabilities?"

"Feed Samantha the list of people who had motives, together with all the background data, and see what she comes up with."

"What about means and opportunity?"

"From what we've seen so far, everybody who got past the entrance guards at the studio had opportunities, and probably everybody had the means. None of what's happened demanded any fancy skills." Josh looked at me. "While you were at your aunt's, I talked to the head electrician on the phone. He was up on the grid while the police checked out where that monitor was hung. The C-clamp had definitely been loosened, and there wasn't a fingerprint on it. Not one. Nor any dust. So the 'accident' was definitely deliberate."

There was a momentary silence as the full import of that sank in on both of us. Then Josh thrust his probability program into Samantha's disk drive and started computing as though lives depended on it.

Samantha flirted with him, blinking her red and green lights, and swallowing up data. Josh cursed. I cleared my throat.

"Wait a minute." I squinted at Samantha's screen. She was pulling her D O E S N O T C O M P U T E nonsense again. I punched a few buttons, looked unwillingly at Josh's data sheet, and keyed some in, establishing a rhythm. "You've got to treat her like a colleague, not an adversary. And don't try to get in a race with her, because Samantha can compute ten times faster than both of us together, and she knows it. Stop hammering at her."

He tried it. Samantha showed off by responding like an angel. "Thanks," Josh said gruffly. He kept keyboarding at the rhythm I had set, and Samantha blinked up her responses, and I leaned back in my chair and wished we'd never gotten into this.

If I hadn't gotten in, Aunt Jane might have been killed.

At last it registered on me that Samantha had shifted out of active mode. Josh pressed PRINT, waited while a sheet of paper scrolled through the printer, then tore it off and held it out to me.

It was the list of prime suspects, in order of Samantha's choice, with the probability ratio stated. Margaret Geller's name led all the rest.

I was silent for so long that Josh said, "Well?" He said it like a challenge, as though he wanted to provoke a fight. I felt too tired; in fact I felt shaky. I looked at the paper and I kept seeing Margaret Geller's face at the moment she burst through those metal doors, after Jane Palmer Kirby had destroyed Celia in full view of a couple of million viewers. And earlier, when Aunt Jane had reminded her she no longer had power over story lines, that she no longer had any power at all. I kept remembering what Leslie had said about a long-gone husband and a freaked-out daughter.

"I feel sorry for her," I said slowly.

Josh looked at me as if I were the world's most total idiot. "You feel sorry for her! When she may have darn near killed you? When she could kill yet?"

"That's just it—" I fought back tears. They put me at a disadvantage, and that made me angry. "We're not just messing around with computer fraud this time. Oh, I know, it sounds . . . *exciting* . . . 'computer detectives.' But this is different. And anyway," I finished illogically, "nobody's been killed."

Josh's face changed. "Look, Sidney," he said gently, "we've got to face it. Sooner or later, if we keep on in this kind of work, we're bound to be faced with identifying a murderer. We may be facing that now."

"It's easy for you to talk. You're so logical and detached. *I* can't help seeing . . . a gas chamber, or an electric chair, or something."

Josh's eyes blazed. "You think just because I don't go around making a big thing of my feelings that I don't care? *I* know what can happen if we provide proof against a criminal! I thought of it a lot earlier than you did, because I *am* logical. That doesn't mean the thought of bringing someone to a death sentence or life imprisonment doesn't turn my stomach! You don't have to be 'tuned in' and 'sensitive to vibrations,'" he mimicked savagely, "to feel sick about that! So stop patting yourself on the back for being more sensitive than other people, and save some compassion for the criminal's victims!"

We stared at each other, shaken.

"I'm sorry," I said at last, in a cracked voice. "I just never thought — I mean —"

"You didn't think. Just leave it at that." Josh no longer sounded angry. "I guess," he said slowly, "what we have to hold on to is that we're not judge and jury. We're investigators. And all we have any business investigating for is the truth. We're not hackers; we're not fudging data for or against anybody. And we don't *make* anyone innocent or guilty. After that, it's . . . over to higher authorities."

It was the longest speech I could ever remember hearing Josh make. It was also the most naked. Josh was always so careful to preserve scientific impartiality. He turned away toward the window and thrust his hands deep in his pockets.

I sat there contemplating my own weaknesses. Josh was right, of course. That was why we were a good combination, we balanced each other out. And if Margaret Geller was The Joker, all my pity, all my compassion, wouldn't help her or anyone else as much as stopping her before she played a joke again.

"What do you think we should do next?" I asked in as normal a voice as I could manage.

"Take Samantha to the studio tomorrow. If anything does go on, her Special Services skills could come in handy." He was referring to the way we'd caught Dad's computer theft by rigging Samantha to send off alarm bells and smoke signals when the thief swung into action.

"Agreed."

"And be at the studio by whatever time

your aunt shows up there. I don't have much faith in your dad or any other doctor being able to dissuade her."

"Also agreed."

"And," Josh said reluctantly, "you'd better look at the statistics on the other suspects."

Samantha had signaled Ross Taylor as her second choice.

"I don't like it," I said in that same effortful voice, "but you're right. We have to know."

"Right." Josh put his hand on my shoulder. "We don't, however, have to tell your aunt about any of this unless it turns out to be necessary. Anyway, Margaret Geller far and away leads the pack." He reached in his pocket for a handkerchief. "Come on, blow your nose and wipe your eyes and let's get back to work."

He put his arm around me as I obeyed the first two directions, and then he put the other arm around me. But it was a good ten minutes before work got our attention.

There were good-natured jeers when we emerged at last into the war room, but they ended quickly. Cordelia looked at our faces and kicked Steve, but it hadn't been necessary because he'd been looking, too. Ceegee cleared his throat.

"Well, you guys, we have one ray of sunshine for you. The correlation of twenty years' worth of *Lust for Life* plots with ratings shares is done. So's the data on relationships between characters — boy, is that almost Freudian at times! — and the character changes."

"Consistent or otherwise," Cordelia put in. "Plus I have a list of characters who were written out in ways that could justify their reappearance."

"What about that data I dug up on the competition?" Josh asked.

"Still in the works. Maybe we could have it ready by tomorrow night, if we all cut school," Steve said happily.

"Skip the sacrifice. I don't want it on my conscience if you all flunk out. By the end of the week should do just fine," I told him.

"I do have a tentative list of all-time ratings winners." Ceegee reached for a printout. "Murder, rape, seduction, natural catastrophe, unnatural catastrophe, trial scenes, scandals. Oh, yes, and weddings. Audiences love weddings."

"In other words, all the network would have to do is aim the cameras at backstage —" I couldn't help it; all at once I started to giggle. I laughed and laughed, until Cordelia in alarm put her arms around me, and Josh steered me to a chair.

"It's just culture shock, from all this TV world immersion," he said blandly. "Maybe it's time we all went home."

Which wasn't a bad idea, considering it was now midnight and Josh and I planned to be at the studio at five a.m.

We made it, too, not over my mother's dead body but thanks to her chauffeuring. Mother was torn between wanting to stay and hover over her sister, and being afraid that if she did she'd blow our cover. She solaced herself by remembering Josh's skill in the martial arts. As for Josh, he was falling all over himself apologizing to us for not preventing Friday's accident.

"Josh," Mother said at last, "nobody expects you to be Superman."

We had some trouble getting Samantha past the security guards, until Aunt Jane arrived and vouched for her. Aunt Jane was in a wheelchair and chafing to get out of it. Upstairs in the offices, typewriters were chattering out today's script changes under Leslie's supervision. Her husband had driven her in, and he *was* staying.

I gave Leslie Cordelia's list of surefire crowd pleasers. "She's not far wrong," Leslie said wryly. "That girl could have a career in TV serials." She also took the list of characters that could be resurrected, for future study.

Painters were painting sets. Somebody was hauling draperies down from those racks far overhead. Tom Shea and his crew were supervising the removal of shabby furniture, to make way for new items coming in.

"By next week, we'll have finished major redecoration of three running sets," Aunt Jane said. She looked remarkably collected and in control, so long as you didn't look too closely around her eyes.

At seven o'clock the cast began arriving. Everyone looked nervous; everyone looked surprised and relieved to find Jane present. They did not look quite so relieved when Mr. Doyle showed, too. He was playing it a bit too brisk and hearty, I thought, observing with a directorial eye. But he did make a good speech, and he kept it brief, stressing again that no further immediate cast changes were anticipated, that the security staff continued to be beefed up, and that he was sure everyone would cooperate with the police. I saw glances exchanged at that.

Aunt Jane followed with the announcement of Leslie Swayne's taking over as head writer "at least for the next three months." Leslie knew the show, and she clearly was well liked and trusted. Which was interesting, I thought, considering the rumors that had reached me earlier of Celia's twistedness rubbing off. It occurred to me we'd better track that rumor to its source. We'd better track all the backstage rumors to their sources, or one common source. Rumor, as I'd learned in school and summer camp, could be like a beast with many heads; as soon as you lopped one off, two more grew in. Only I had a pretty good idea, didn't I, of who was the body (not to mention brains) behind this particular Hydra?

I didn't have an opportunity to share these

gems of insight, because Josh was busy rigging up Samantha before a small but select admiring audience. Fortunately, Samantha looked like any ordinary, expensive SMN computer — her "special features" were concealed inside a standard-issue pearl white exterior. Samantha sat in her office looking beautiful, blinking coquettishly, and when nobody was looking Josh pocketed one necessary chip so nobody could try her out in our absence.

In the studios, the dry runs for today's regular taping and for the special scenes to be inserted in today's broadcast, were taking place. The special scenes were transferred to the sound stage first. Leslie had managed them skillfully — a prologue that was actually a flashback excerpted from the tape of the live broadcast, showing Celia's death. Someone trying to reach her on the telephone (in full view of spectators, so the person could still be part of the list of suspects). Her lover, hammering on the door of her apartment (also with witnesses). Her apartment super, bringing a master key, discovering the body. The arrival of the police. All this would be interspersed with the scenes already in the can, of River Edge going about its business. Since six o'clock, the director and editors had been going over the tapes, deleting and splicing, leaving spaces for insertions, according to the master script Leslie and Aunt Jane had produced.

The new scenes were shot quickly — for editing needs, and so the sound stage would be free for the regularly scheduled taping. All this while typewriters kept clattering out new script. Josh kept chumming with the technicians — and even, I noticed admiringly, with the police. Two of the plainclothes detectives were back. Josh also managed to nail Mr. Doyle for a private chat. And I kept circulating — mouth shut, eyes peeled, and both ears flapping. And all antennas tuned. I made the rounds, being careful not to establish any order — dressing rooms, makeup room, green room (where today's bit players and under fivers clammed up quickly at my entrance). Offices, design rooms, technical rooms. Coffee area (where the same thing happened). Sound stage (whenever the red light wasn't on). I kept watching all the entrance doors.

Josh and I had lunch in our "office," with the monitor's sound turned up just in case the soundproofing didn't work. "I pumped Mr. Doyle on Geller," Josh said. "He doesn't know her well, because he's only had this job for three years, but he's heard plenty. He doubts she's The Joker, but not that she's a full-blown neurotic and a first class witch. You should hear what the boys in the boardroom call her. It's a lot stronger than Dragon Lady." He wouldn't repeat the phrase for my tender ears.

"I keep expecting her to walk in here," I

said, "after what she pulled yesterday at my aunt's. She doesn't know, does she, that Aunt Jane's on the job? She certainly didn't look as if she would be, yesterday. And she doesn't know," I went on, mixing pronouns with abandon, "that Leslie's taking over her job."

"Mr. Doyle told the media that Ms. Kirby was 'resting comfortably, and would be back with the show in the near future,'" Josh corroborated. "He figured the less actual facts given out, the better. And he also," Josh added acidly, "undoubtedly figures that the less the public knows, the more avid they'll be to tune in for further developments."

"Exactly. And nobody in the company knew about Leslie's new assignment, until Aunt Jane announced it. Nobody knew Aunt Jane was coming in."

"Except possibly Ross Taylor, to both of those."

"Unless he's not telling us everything he knows. Okay, I know that's possible. What I'm getting at is what, given what we know about Margaret Geller, would she be most likely to do under those circumstances?"

Josh looked at me. "Show up to be the Earth Mother coming to the rescue of her poor show, nobly rising above how deeply she's been hurt."

"You've got it. Except — where is she?"

Josh frowned. "I don't like it," he said decidedly. "You wait here."

"Don't try to park me. What are you going to do?"

"Ask Mr. Doyle to find out whether anyone's talked to Geller. And tell the lieutenant maybe he'd better find out where she is."

We did both those things. We were greeted with a degree of respect that told me we might be very much on the right track. And then we waited.

Mr. Doyle telephoned the Geller apartment. No one answered. The lieutenant had words with the security guards at the downstairs entrance. Ms. Geller had not been seen. Around us, the daily routine, greatly accelerated, swirled on.

At three o'clock, Aunt Jane called an hour's time out so that everyone could watch today's show being aired. She had already, I noticed, made some changes and tightened the familiar lead-in. There was a rapid fire montage of scenes, to a considerably jazzed-up version of the theme song. The show began, with a shockingly distorted view of Celia's body, lying on the floor, the face destroyed. A cut to the shattered fragments of the music box. And then — my skin crawled. Aunt Jane and Leslie had inserted a shot of the dead rat, as though it had been left in Celia's room as a murderer's calling card.

The show rolled on. The staccato interspersing of everyday activity with frenzy worked; it really worked. I could feel the company draw a collective sigh of relief. When the sign off came, everyone was feeling considerably better.

"Okay!" the director shouted. "Scene 8C; Brannigan house. Dress!"

As the actors moved toward their stations, I saw Josh's lieutenant friend walking purposefully towards Mr. Doyle. A few minutes later, Jack Doyle joined us, his face tight.

"You were right on target about keeping an eye on Margaret Geller. But you were wrong about the reason. She's not The Joker; she's the target. Somebody gassed her after giving her doped cigarettes. Which could have been done earlier by anyone who knew her. Jane tells me everyone here knows how many packs a day she smokes, and she arrived here that last day with a full new carton. There was a new just-opened pack by her bed, and all the packs left in the carton were doped up, too. It wasn't a suicide attempt. There's clear evidence her apartment was broken into in the night."

Chapter 12

All at once, what had seemed a fairly clear picture was all distorted.

Josh found his voice first. "Suicide *attempt?* Then she isn't dead?"

"She's alive — and very lucky. She was found just in time. It's a good thing," Mr. Doyle said tautly, "that somebody got worried."

"Somebody? Wait a minute," I said slowly, "you don't mean she was just found *now*, because we got worried? Because how could she have been inhaling gas that long and survive? You said the break-in was at night!"

"She was found around eight o'clock this morning." Mr. Doyle lit a cigarette nervously, remembered smoking was forbidden on the sound stage, and snubbed it out. "She'd agreed to a breakfast interview with a reporter. In fact, she told him to be sure and keep ringing the doorbell until she answered, because she was going to take something the night before to make sure she'd sleep."

"So The Joker's cleverness with the cigarettes was unnecessary." Josh was concentrating hard. "Go on."

"When the reporter couldn't rouse her, he got the super, who unlocked the door. Exit Ms. Geller to Columbia Presbyterian Hospital. Her place isn't far from there, up on Riverside Drive. That's why the detectives on the Joker case didn't know about it. Different precinct. They just found out now when they started checking." He left us to tell the news to my aunt.

I felt as if the "sure and firm-set earth" beneath my feet had turned to quicksand, or whatever it was in that quotation from *Macbeth* that my English teacher'd hammered into me.

"We'd better talk," Josh said in an odd voice. I nodded. We exited the sound stage, where the news was traveling rapidly, and made for our dressing-room office and Samantha. Josh put the crucial chip back into her while I sat and tried to get my head together.

"We've been seeing everything all twisted," I said. "Aunt Jane wasn't The Joker's target. *Lust for Life* wasn't the target — except as means to an end. The target was Margaret Geller."

"Maybe we were seeing it twisted because

we were meant to," Josh said thoughtfully.

"You mean a smoke screen?"

"Exactly. Or an illusion. There's lots of illusion around a TV studio," Josh said with distaste. "And who'd know better how to create them than the pros?"

"It wouldn't have to be someone from the industry. Geller has a lot of past history that's pretty murky."

"Like the long-lost husband, and the daughter." Josh unlocked his attache. "I just happen," he added, "to have brought along my black book."

"When are you going to get that thing booby-trapped against theft or intruders?" I inquired. I was only half joking. Josh just nodded. He was already connecting up wires.

"Go tell Linda I need a telephone set in here, and to keep the line open for me. There's a jack underneath the counter; I checked."

Usually that lord-of-the-manor tone makes my hackles rise, but it didn't matter now. Electronic spying was Josh's department, and he could have it. Anyway, I had other fish to fry. I delivered Josh's message to Linda and brought back the phone set, then I tracked down Leslie.

"Who would know the most about Ms. Geller, going way, way back?"

"Helen Windermere," she said immediately. "They worked in radio together."

That was the gracious actress, who played

Caroline Armitage, I'd had lunch with once. I found her where I'd met her then, in the design office, sipping a cup of tea. She remembered me, and smiled. "Hello dear. Are you looking for a quiet place, too?" She looked tired, older than she had before. "Would you like some tea? I have tea bags with me — Lapsang Souchong, Earl Grey?"

"No, thank you — yes, please." I realized I could use some. "Mrs. Windermere, may I talk with you a while?"

"Of course, dear."

"About Margaret Geller."

She looked grave and sad, but not surprised. "Of course," she said again, and indicated a ball-wheeled chair. I pulled it over.

"I've heard she made a lot of enemies. I need to know who they are."

She didn't pretend she didn't know what I meant, or why. "Enemies go with the territory when anyone has that much power. Not that Margaret cared. Sometimes I thought —" She stopped.

"That she gloried in it?"

"You could say that. She loved power, and she loved testing it and proving it. Of course," Helen Windermere added quickly, "she really believed that when she manipulated people it was for their own good. Or for the show's good. In her eyes, that came first, and she always felt she was the only one who knew what was right for *Lust*."

"Like the degeneration of Celia's character?"

She nodded. "None of us wanted to lose Leslie from the cast, but Jane Kirby was right. The Celia story line was ruining the show. Even Leslie knew it."

But not Margaret Geller. I stared into space and tried to make pieces fit together. "The tension around here ... the sicker-than-normal tension ... do you think that came from Celia's character and story? Or from The Joker?" What I really meant was which came first, the chicken or the egg?

"I've always thought," Helen Windermere said surprisingly, "that it came from Margaret."

"You've known her for a long time, haven't you?"

She nodded. "You know the expression, 'Nature abhors a vacuum'? Something in Margaret abhorred a calm. We used to say, if things were going too well, 'Watch out — Margaret's going to blow!'"

"And people got hurt, didn't they? People lost jobs."

"She's a creature of impulse. Please, don't get a one-sided picture. Margaret can be surprisingly kind. She lashes out, then she makes amends. Look how she went over to Jane Kirby's apartment to take care of her, after the big scene here earlier." So that visit was now common knowledge. "She fired Ross

Taylor years ago, in a fit of temper, and two years later she insisted on hiring him again. He's worked with her regularly ever since."

"I need to know who else she's treated that way. And the people she *didn't* make amends to. Even if it's only rumor."

I thought she'd balk. To my astonishment she regarded me searchingly for several minutes, then reached in her handbag for a pen and pad. She wrote for some time, then tore off the sheets and handed them to me.

I went back to the dressing room-office and found it locked, although I could hear Samantha humming. I knocked, and Josh disengaged his extra-special lock and let me in.

"Here. The Margaret Geller Special Enemies and Victims List." It wasn't until then that I saw Mrs. Windermere had included the names of Margaret's husband and the daughter. I wondered what she knew that we didn't, yet. Josh saw them, too, and whistled.

"I've turned up deep data that adds up with some of this already," Josh said. "Sit down, Sidney. You're going to read this whether you want to or not."

He ripped off a printout, and there was something in his face that made me fold up into the chair, made me take the paper as he held it out.

ALBERT GELLER: BORN ZURICH, SWITZERLAND MAY 13, 1919. ARR. N.Y.

OCT. 11, 1934. NAT. CTZN.
U. S. ARMY 1942–1945.
HON. DISG. DEC. 11, 1945.
M. MARGARET DAVIS, AUG.
20, 1946. DIV. FEB. 26,
1959. D. DENVER, COLO.
FEB. 7, 1979.

"I could have been an arranged disappearance."

"It could have been an arranged disappearoddly.

CAROLE ANN GELLER:
BORN CHICAGO MARCH 27,
1948. ARRESTS: (1) DOWNERS GROVE, ILL. (ARSON)
FEB. 19, 1960: FANNINGSBURG JUV. TREATMENT
CTR. (F'BURG, ILL.) 1960–
1962; 1963–1966; (2) MILWAUKEE, WIS. (RUNAWAY)
OCT. 17, 1963; (3) NEW
YORK, N.Y. (CONTROLLED
SUBSTANCE) JULY 5, 1966;
(4) NEW YORK, N.Y. (ATTEMPTED SUICIDE) JAN.
2, 1967; WHITESTONE
HOUSE CLINIC, UTICA,
N.Y., JAN.–JUNE, 1967.
D. AUG. 28, 1968 (BARBITURATES).

Pity stung my eyes. Not just for Carole
Geller, but for her mother. I felt Josh's own

black gaze on me steadily, but when I looked up its focus on me had broken." I got into her visitor records at the clinic," Josh said.

"How did you — No, wait." I frowned. "1967. That's a long time back. How come records from then are stored in a main frame computer now?"

"That's what I wondered. The clinic seems to have computerized all back case records that have been needed since they went electronic. Needed because patients were re-admitted — *or* because requests for data have come through."

"Somebody's been looking into Carole's records."

"Right. Plural. The first was Margaret Geller, who got a court order under the Freedom of Information Act. The second was someone who'd been a patient at the clinic, at the same time Carole was, also via court order, on the same grounds: relationship."

I looked down at the next entry on the printout.

The blood drummed in my ears.

"Look, Sidney," Josh said at last, in a voice I rarely heard him use. "You can't close your eyes to it. What it means, we can't prove, but you can put two and two together as well as I can."

Or the police. The police were going to be poking into everything, now that The Joker and the Geller murder attempt had been linked.

I heard Josh rise. "I'll go tell the detectives," he said quietly.

"No."

"Webster, don't be stupid. We can't sit on this. And it won't go away by your sticking your head in the sand."

"I'm not sticking my head. I'm just not going to have us stick out our necks." I couldn't explain in any words that Josh would understand, so I took refuge in diversion. "I shouldn't think you'd want to advertise that you've been hacking in official records —"

Josh's eyebrow rose and that little muscle by his left temple began to twitch. "If you're going to start preaching about ethics —"

"Don't *you* preach them to me. We're not licensed investigators, so the police can't pull our licenses. They'll uncover this anyway, sooner or later. I just want it to be a little later." Josh opened his mouth and I went on, hard and cold. "*I* signed the contract to do this investigating. I signed a contract of confidentiality. And *you* signed a contract of confidentiality with SSW Enterprises, when you agreed to work for me."

The words hung in the air, and my blood hammered, and Josh and I stared at each other. At last he said, very distinctly, "Twenty-four hours. After that you know what you can do with that damn contract. And you'd better know what you intend to do about the rest of it."

He started punching buttons on Samantha. She squawked in protest but for once, surprisingly, did not tell him what was on her mind. "What do you think you're doing?" I inquired, in as natural a voice as I could manage.

"Going home. To work with the rest of your slaves on the market research we were hired for. The sooner that's finished, the sooner we'll be out of this charade." Josh slammed his black book and program disks into his attache case, snapped it shut, and walked out.

I was left with the printout, staring unseeingly through troubled eyes as in the vague distance Samantha's red and green lights blinked an accusation.

Chapter 13

I shut down Samantha and went out, locking her and the printout in carefully. I went down the red-carpeted corridor, found my aunt and spoke to her carefully, and after that I phoned my mother. I went through all these motions like a zombie, a fact my mother immediately picked up.

"Are you all right? Is Jane all right? What happened? Is Josh going to stay in the city tonight, too?"

"Yes. Yes. I'm not sure. Ms. Geller was found in her apartment overcome by gas, and the place had been broken into. Josh has gone home."

There was a brief, significant silence. "Would you like me to come in?" Mother asked gently. "Or your father?"

"I'll call you if we need you," I said guardedly. I knew she would pick up on the use of the plural pronoun.

After that I tottered out and watched the

rest of the day's taping. Josh was conspicuous by his absence, at least to me. The atmosphere around the studio was odd. I had expected murmurs, and rumors, and apprehension. Instead, the gathering places of the company were strangely silent. It was as if The Joker, and Margaret Geller, had become forbidden subjects. Everything was low key, and slowly it began to percolate through my misery that there were two contradictory currents eddying, faint but *there*. One was shock and a kind of numb horror, but the other, very definitely, was relief.

Was everybody present sure that (a) Margaret Geller was The Joker and (b) the gassing had been a suicide attempt? It did not make sense. Or did they simply not care if there had been attempted murder?

Announcements emerged from the front office periodically. Margaret Geller was "resting comfortably." The network, and/or sponsor, had managed to get the whole affair very much played down where public consumption was concerned. The sponsor was *very* pleased with the reception of the live broadcast and accompanying story line surgery. In the late afternoon a changing of the guard occurred as the early-morning shift of performers began to leave and the late shift drifted in. Office personnel and designers began closing down.

Aunt Jane was staying through. The director and his staff were staying through. The Swaynes were staying through.

At six p.m. Bill Swayne collared me. "I've just kidnapped my wife for dinner. You're coming, too." We went to a little Indonesian restaurant over on Broadway, and we did not talk about the show at all. Bill told about college escapades, and about growing up in a little town in Wisconsin, and I sat there growing more and more unhappy.

Back at the studio, the evening's routine was much like the morning's. It was nearly eleven p.m. before Aunt Jane and I, the last ones out, took a taxi to the Upper West Side.

"I'm getting undressed, and then I'm having some soup. Make yourself at home. Borrow anything you want in the way of robe and nightgown." Aunt Jane disappeared into her bathroom. She limped out some time later, wrapped in her Chinese robe, to find me still sitting somberly.

"I'd advise a hot bath. What do you want then? Split pea, minestrone, or plain old-fashioned chicken soup?" Aunt Jane opened the freezer door on a series of fat plastic containers.

"I'll do that. You get off your leg." All day, somehow, what with everything else, our wounded conditions had totally slipped my mind. "Did you make all this in your spare time? You're as bad as Mom."

"Not I. That's Margaret Geller's handiwork. Believe it or not, she sent it over while I was in the hospital, and my cleaning woman got it safely stowed away."

My hand stopped in mid air.

"Can't we send out for pizza or Chinese food? This neighborhood's crawling with all-night restaurants, isn't it?"

"If you'd rather, but it seems a shame —" Aunt Jane's face changed. "Sidney, you don't think there's anything wrong with the soup? After Margaret herself was attacked?"

"That doesn't mean she couldn't have been The Joker. Aunt Jane, we need to talk."

Aunt Jane looked at me. She went to the telephone. "Get undressed," she said. "I'll call out for something."

I dragged it out as long as I could. I even took a shower. When I emerged, swathed in Chinese red velour, my aunt was waiting for me gravely on the sofa.

"What have you found out? This isn't just about Josh, is it? I heard he left."

I didn't get into that. "How much do you know about Ross Taylor?"

Whatever she was expecting, it wasn't that. She did a double take, then something shut behind her eyes. "I know he's a very good, dependable actor with a good following in the twenty-seven to thirty-five-year-old viewership. And he's loyal. He's stayed with *Lust* in spite of several offers elsewhere."

"Did you know he turned down a prime

time pilot? And he's been saying no to good offers from that other soap he used to be on?" She hadn't known; I knew that right away. She looked disconcerted and then, heartbreakingly, she blushed. I steeled myself. "It wasn't because of you. Not *just* because of you. It couldn't have been. Because the same kind of thing was going on before you came on the show. He'd be at the point of signing somewhere else. Once he even *did* sign, and started a new character, and when the producers there wanted to renew his contract at a higher salary, he came back to *Lust for Life*. For union scale. He's not making much now, compared to what he's being offered elsewhere — and turning down. It almost sounds like somebody's making him do it, doesn't it?"

"Exactly what are you getting at, Sidney?" Aunt Jane asked deliberately.

Maybe heavy artillery would be kinder. "Did you know he was married to Margaret Geller's daughter Carole when she killed herself? He met her when they were both in a private treatment center. The marriage was a secret. He found her when she OD'd, and called the police, but not soon enough for them to save her. A year later he started to drop everything and come running, every time that Margaret Geller whistled."

All at once I wished, passionately, that I hadn't started any of this. Me and my intuition, my wanting to protect. Josh was right, we should have kept everything clean and above-board and — detached.

"Hand me the telephone," my aunt said, in a voice like ice. She called Ross Taylor, still in that crystal voice, and told him to get over right away.

He and the Szechuan beef arrived together.

"Tell him," my aunt ordered. She seemed to have withdrawn into herself, like some shelled sea creature.

I couldn't say it all again. I handed him the relevant part of the printout, and he read it. When he finished he, like Aunt Jane, had aged. But he also seemed, in a strange way, relieved.

"I was going to tell you." He was talking, very definitely, strictly to Aunt Jane. "There wasn't any reason to, in the beginning, and lately there have been too many reasons. Pro and con."

He searched through his pockets unsuccessfully. Aunt Jane took out cigarettes and matches and tossed them toward him, while I tried to make myself invisible.

"Thanks." He offered her one, which she refused, and lit his own. "I met Carole in Whitestone. I wasn't there for drugs. I was recovering from clinical depression, courtesy of Margaret Geller. She fired me because I'd dared to have a beard without consulting her, and she started rumors I had a drug problem. So I could understand very well what had set that poor kid on a destructive path that culminated in a suicide attempt. I suppose I thought I could rehabilitate her with understanding," Ross said bitterly, "and Carole had found herself an all-protecting parent figure. She was nineteen, and she was beautiful, and so — fragile. Just like the little-girl Celia that was written into flashbacks."

For a minute we all were silent. Then Ross shrugged.

"I'll make it brief. I was discharged first. I went back on visits. The doctors wouldn't release Carole without someone around to keep an eye out, and Margaret wouldn't have her. So I took her in. When Carole started having nightmares that I'd desert her as her father had, we got married, secretly. Neither of us wanted the Dragon Lady to know. I was afraid Carole would slip back on amphetamines and barbiturates if we didn't marry. What I didn't know was that she already had."

He stubbed out his cigarette. "That year was a roller coaster between heaven and hell. I realized, by spring, that Carole was seriously ill. She tried suicide, twice. Maybe she didn't mean to die, maybe it was a cry for help. *I* don't know."

"But it wasn't reported," I said, not moving.

For the first time, he looked at me. "No, it wasn't. Margaret was threatening to have her committed, and Carole swore she'd kill herself if that happened . . . so I was the keeper. I got very good at telling when she got hold of pills, and when she took too many. There's a change in the breathing. By summer," Ross said harshly, "I was getting thoroughly sick of playing God. I simply couldn't care any more." He shook his head. "Maybe I got careless. That last day we had a terrible fight — Carole accused me of not caring, of using her just as everyone else in her whole life had. She meant her parents, of course. I had signed for a Broadway play, and she was trying to make me miss rehearsal. I went to the rehearsal, and I don't know to this day whether I'd noticed that breathing change before I left, or not. I went out for food after with other members of the cast, and then I went for a walk. When I got home, it was too late."

"And Margaret threatened to make you responsible."

"She could have done it," Ross said. He found himself in front of a chair and threw himself down. "She'd planted those drug rumors earlier, and she knew the police had been interested. When she found out I was the one who'd discovered Carole too late, *I* was the one who'd robbed her of her baby. It didn't matter that *she* hadn't wanted the Carole that was, just the one she dreamed up in her own head. I'd stolen something that was hers. She started digging, and then she came up with the marriage. And then she started —"

"I can fill in the rest," Aunt Jane said. It was the first she's spoken. "Innuendos. A hint to the police here, to a gossip columnist there. Not a good image for the sponsors' products. And then — elaboration on the script? Overtones not of carelessness but of murder?"

"I couldn't afford it," Ross said bitterly. "Not at that point. I was at that point between young love roles and distinguished leads, and actors in that category are a dime a dozen. I thought I'd stick with *Lust* for a year or so until I got better known. But the better I was known, the more damage she could do. I was a coward. Then *you* came on the show, and I no longer wanted to leave."

He looked straight at my aunt. "I was going to, though. I'd reached the point of thinking if we were to have any future, I would have to. I was about to tell Margaret Geller exactly where she could go . . . and then — The Joker."

I didn't know what that meant — whether he created The Joker, or The Joker appeared as if heaven-sent. He was telling Aunt Jane, "At first, I actually was relieved. I knew the tricks would drive you into doing something. And I was pretty sure it would mean sacking Geller. I knew how Margaret's mind worked, and I knew she was working all of her convoluted relationship with Carole out through

Celia. I knew if it came to a showdown between the two of you, my darling, you
wouldn't let Margaret win. Not over you, not
over the show. But I never thought Margaret
would try to harm you. And *I* did not harm
her."

"You should have told me," Aunt Jane
said. "*All* of it."

They'd forgotten I was in the room. It was
time for me to get out of there, and I did so,
creeping away on little cat feet. I had soul
and mind searching of my own to do. For in
spite of everything — and that included not
being sure whether he was or was not The
Joker — I did not believe he had tried to kill
Margaret Geller.

Chapter 14

I fell asleep before Ross Taylor left. I awoke while it was still dark. Every bone in my body ached, and a faint light arrowed from the direction of the kitchen. The hands of the clock stood at a few minutes after four.

Aunt Jane was at the kitchen's miniscule table, already dressed. "I want to be at the studio before five, if possible. You can take a cab down later."

"I'll be ready." I snatched a bagel from the table and went to dress. I was able to climb into slacks and sweater, brush my hair and anchor it up with a barette, and still have time for a glass of orange juice. Neither of us spoke much, in the apartment or in the cab downtown. Once Aunt Jane said, "Ross is going to tell that police lieutenant about Carole," and I said, "Good." Once I asked, "Is Margaret Geller out of the hospital yet?" and she said, "Not as of last night. They expect to keep her a day or so." That was all.

It was dark and cold when the cab skidded to a stop before the deserted, warehouse-looking building. No, not deserted. A figure emerged from the shadows of the steps where it had been sitting. Josh.

He didn't say anything about yesterday. He didn't act as if we'd quarreled. He said, in an absolutely colorless voice, "I cracked into some police records on George Albert Geller's death. It could be fishy."

"What do you mean?" Aunt Jane came back, so fast I knew she was grasping at straws. So her heart might be sure about Ross Taylor, but some corner of her mind was not.

"He died in a fire in a dump of an apartment building. At least the body was presumed to be his. Look, do we have to stand out here? The security guys aren't here yet, and the place is locked up tight."

"I have a key." Aunt Jane produced it, and we trooped inside, after she had manipulated the alarm system with another, smaller key. We walked up the bleak cement steps with their plumber's-pipe railings, past the props dump and company-congregating areas, now swallowed up in shadows. Aunt Jane unlocked her office door, and flipped on the switch. The overhead light shone down mercilessly on the three of us.

Josh looked, if possible, worse than we did. He was even rumpled. "Did you get any sleep?" I exclaimed involuntarily.

"I was up all night hacking. And if you tell anyone I admitted that I'll break your neck." Josh turned to my aunt. "Geller started drinking after they broke up."

"Before," Aunt Jane interrupted. "I've heard rumors."

"Could be. The records of his getting in trouble for it started after. He just escaped a serious drunk driving charge, and once or twice he was locked up overnight after getting violent in bars during blackouts. He committed himself for treatment — alternative to going to jail — after tearing apart a neighborhood place in Milwaukee." Josh paused. "He assaulted a woman. He thought she was his wife."

The electric light fell on the decorator-perfect furniture; on Aunt Jane, a haggard parody of herself, in the peacock chair. "What happened?" I asked through dry lips.

"He was in the sanitarium for two months, then was an outpatient for six months after. That was in 1969, about a year after Carole Geller died. Up 'til then," Josh said methodically, "he seems to have held down regular jobs. At least a year to eighteen months at a time. Either job-shopping at engineering, or teaching at small community colleges. After that, it got irregular. Two months' work here, six weeks' worth in another state."

He's been into Social Security records, I thought. I didn't say so.

"His death," Aunt Jane said tightly.

"I'm getting to that. Some time between then and 1979, he got to look at the official records on his daughter. His request for them is recorded. So he knew about Margaret's refusal to authorize Carole's release from Whitestone. And from the looks of things, the lady wasn't anxious to have the girl at home before that, either." Josh sounded angry. "The kid was warehoused, right until she was eighteen and the state couldn't forcibly restrain her any longer. The Dragon Lady must have been one hell of a mother."

"Not according to the way Margaret Geller talked. But I'm not surprised," Aunt Jane said grimly. "Go on about the father."

"That could be a horse of another color. It looks as if what was happening to the kid knocked the stuffing out of him. He hit the skids bad by 1975. Single-room-occupancy hotel rooms, and so forth."

"If he wasn't working, how was he paying the bills?" I asked practically.

"Panhandling, maybe. Or picking up a couple of bucks here and there for odd jobs he didn't report to the IRS." Josh looked at us. "There are things that suggest Margaret sent him sums of money, but I can't prove that. After 1978 Geller was living in a flophouse apartment building in Denver. In early 1979 there wasn't any heat — the pipes burst — tenants used gas stoves to keep warm. You can fill in the rest of it," Josh said heavily. "We see it on TV news in practically every northern city. The building was old, it went like a tinderbox, and people got killed."

"But not Geller. Is that what you're trying to say?" Aunt Jane demanded.

"*Maybe* not Geller. The body of a man about Geller's age and build was found in his apartment, along with a couple of empty liquor bottles. They couldn't make a positive identification," Josh said bluntly, "because the body was too badly charred. But no Geller turned up afterwards, and no other man was unaccounted for. So the death certificate read George Albert Geller."

For a second there was no life in the room but the ticking of the clock, unnaturally loud.

Josh turned to Aunt Jane wearily. "Can you find a way to feed this information to the police without my having to come out and tell them how I got it? *I* wouldn't mind, but I got some of the access numbers I used from other people."

"I can pass it on as a backstage rumor, or via a reporter I know I can trust. You're right; the police should have it." Aunt Jane drew a breath, and I almost saw color returning to her cheeks.

Josh reached in his attache case. "You can have my printout; just don't pass it on. I was able to get a picture of Geller, too." We gazed at it, a likeness from some newspaper morgue, courtesy of electronic technology — a big, sad, shambling sheepdog of a man.

After a minute, Aunt Jane stirred. "I'll get the police onto it." She reached for the telephone with a forced copy of her old brisk manner. Josh and I looked at each other, and with one accord we departed from her presence.

In the corridor, having shut her office door behind us, I turned to Josh. "What now, do you think?"

"I think we'd better batten down the hatches," Josh said grimly. "If Geller *is* The Joker, he could be anywhere. Or anybody. We don't know what he looks like now." I remembered that sad, nondescript face. "And don't forget, he knows a lot about electronic engineering."

"Meaning he could be part of the technical crew." I shook my head, frowning. "Wait a minute. If it *is* Geller, the one place we don't have to worry about further attempts made is here. It would mean Margaret Geller was the target all along. She's no longer part of *Lust for Life*. She couldn't be here anyway; she's in the hospital."

Even as I said that, I saw the flaw. If harming Margaret Geller was the objective, why had the TV monitor fallen on Aunt Jane and me? "Of course," I said aloud, slowly, "he might not have known that she'd been canned."

Josh followed my reasoning and nodded. "He'd know that he'd reached her last night, though. He'd have to. And he'd think she was either in the hospital, or dead. There was no news update in today's early morning editions of the papers; I've checked. And it's too early yet for the morning TV news."

"If she's gone home from the hospital, he could find out."

"That we can check, too." Josh tried the door of the next office, found it unlocked, and helped himself to the telephone. He called Margaret Geller's house, where there was no answer; then the hospital, where he was told the patient was resting comfortably and had not yet been released.

"Okay," Josh said absently, putting down the phone. I knew that look on his face, and my warning signals started going off.

"Exactly what are you thinking of cooking up now?" I demanded.

"Samantha. I want to get her special features primed before any of the union crew gets here to stop me." Josh raced down the corridor. I pelted after. At the corner by the Green Room he swung around and grabbed me.

"Stay out front! Either with your aunt, or on that bench between her office door and the main entrance. It will be another hour at least before the guards get here, and I don't want you back in this rabbit warren alone. I'm going to be running all over the place, wiring Samantha to the special effects."

I stared blankly at his taut face. "You don't think The Joker's going to try something more? *Why*, if Margaret won't be here?" Then a cold prickle started up my spine. "If Geller's shifted the blame for his daughter's death from Margaret alone to the whole show —"

"You're the expert on psychological motivation, not me," Josh said roughly. "But it could happen, couldn't it? Especially if The Joker's started freaking out?"

"Yes, it could. It was *Lust for Life* that had always been Margaret Geller's greatest interest and best loved creation. And that would explain the dropped TV monitor, wouldn't it?"

Josh was watching me closely. "Another thing. We don't *know* that The Joker's George Albert Geller. There's still Ross Taylor. And other possibilities." He interpreted the look on my face correctly. "Let's not fight now. There isn't time. Sidney, please, go back out front and stay where you're safe. And call me on the house phone the minute any of the crew arrive."

I went, not because I was giving in, but because I had reasons of my own, and the bright montages of cast members' photos watched me as I walked soundlessly back along the carpeted red corridor.

It was all so silent. And dark. And cold. Aunt Jane's door was still closed, and a lighted button on the nearest phone showed she was still using an outside line. Arguing with the police, probably. I sat down on the dark green leatherette of the banquette, and solitude engulfed me like a shroud. Only one bare light bulb, dangling beneath a green metal work shade, broke the dimness. The all-purpose work area was thick with shadows, and crowded with "theater ghosts."

I leaned back against the banquette and closed my eyes, letting the ghosts slip like smoke into my consciousness. This was what had been missing, and had been wrong. Ever since this job began, we had been so rushed there had been no time for thinking. Or for non-thinking; tapping in to intuition. . . . I felt my muscles relaxing, felt myself drifting into that waking dream state that Dad called Alpha consciousness.

Dad is the scientist; Dad could provide the rational explanation. I only knew my best insights, my best work, came when I let myself "go with the current," and up 'til now I hadn't had the chance.

I surrendered myself, as a swimmer does, to the cresting wave, and the theater ghosts came closer and developed faces. Aunt Jane; Margaret Geller; her sad, shambling husband; a tense, unfamiliar young girl's face that I connected unquestioningly with Carole Geller; Ross Taylor; Leslie Swayne, and with her a montage of Celias: bewildered, childlike, tender and nurturing, malevolent, contorted with rage.

All at once I was seeing, as though on a VCR, a series of scenes from *Lust for Life.*

Celia, finding the dead rat. Celia, on the floor all bloody, from the explosion. (I heard Aunt Jane's voice, from the story conference: "If we end the scene that way, no one can be sure whether she's dead or not." And Cordelia: "Characters who are supposed to be dead are always being resurrected.")

And then the Monday show, the montage Leslie had skillfully contrived after she and Cordelia and I had talked: Celia's bloodied body; the shards of the music box; the dead rat, left like a murderer's calling card; the telephone in Celia's apartment ringing, ringing; a man's hand, hammering on the apartment door; an apartment superintendent, summoned to break in with a master key, finding Celia's body —

I was still in that waking trance, but I was suddenly sitting up straight and rigid, and the computer that was my brain was working rapidly. That scene was familiar, so familiar. And not just because I'd helped plan it, watched it rehearsed, seen it on the air. There was another familiarity as well. A picture flashed back: Mr. Doyle, smoking nervously, telling us about the discovery yesterday of Margaret Geller, drugged and gassed.

Something had bothered me at the time, hadn't it? Something had been bothering me all along, not letting me accept whatever seemed the obvious, logical facts. Because they *were* obvious, and something more —

"Theatrical," I whispered. That was it,

wasn't it? Everything that had happened since we'd been here — no, even earlier, in Aunt Jane's account of the show's problems — had been larger than life, like something from a script. Critics said soap operas weren't like life; Cordelia said they were real life hyped up and condensed; here on these sound stages, life was mimicking soap opera scripts.

And why not? that little voice of my irrational self whispered in my brain. In the tight, closed world of the *Lust for Life* company were masters of the genre. People who could play outlandish story lines (like Celia's) and make them real. People who were capable of creating illusions in real life, and making them believable.

People who could create airtight alibis, and red herrings, and false trails . . . and alter time, and conjure characters out of thin air, and make them flesh and blood. People who could, as I was doing now, see plots in their head, whole and complete, a pattern for revenge. Who could, like Celia, become possessed by an "evil demon."

I knew, by now, the persons who could do that, and who had reason. I saw their faces in the mist inside my head, and George Albert Geller's was not among them. One face stood out, stronger than others, in the mist. I looked at it, and knew it, and was not afraid. Only very, very sad.

I knew something else, too. Something was

going to happen today, if we did not stop it — another illusion, and probably a death. *Repetitive patterns*, Cordelia's voice (speaking of classic soap plots) said in my brain. I found myself looking at the metal doors of the sound stage; looking *through* them, and up, at the grid with its lights and poles, high overhead.

The grid had to be checked, the C-clamps had to be checked, and before anyone got here. It could not be left to the crew, who would be arriving any minute. Leslie would be arriving any minute, for a scheduled pre-rehearsal conference with Aunt Jane, if she was not here already.

I shut my mind off from that, concentrated on the image of the grid, and thought hard. Josh? He was still working on Samantha, or he would be here. The clock above the time-card machine was ticking inexorably. I was wearing navy blue slacks and sweater, the next thing to invisibility. I slid out of my shoes, and in my stockinged feet went soundlessly across the shabby vinyl floor to the metal doors.

They were not locked. They did not creak as I tested them cautiously, then slipped inside. Here, too, only one faint work light glowed. It showed, mere rims of glimmer, the ladder bars bolted to the near left wall. They led up, up, to the grid and the narrow ledge where the drapery collection hung, and their duplicate led down again on the far wall. Between them stretched an infinity of grids, and lighting bars, and clamps, and dangling poles.

I gripped the ladder bar above my head, put my foot on the lowest rung, and tested. It took my weight. Up I went, and up, one hand above the other, and one foot. Don't look down; don't look up; keep going. I came up at last, like a swimmer, into an aerial world.

The grid of heavy pipes spread like a monstrous math chart over the whole sound stage. Six inches above it, a distorted geometric spiderweb, ran a cross hatch of narrow walkways of metal mesh. Their only rails were ropes, running slackly between wide-spaced metal stanchions. Here and there, pipes ran parallel to the grid, some two feet higher than the walkways, but over the spaces between walks and grids. I couldn't see what held them; I could see almost nothing except vague graphic shapes and glints of metal where black paint had flaked off. Red light glowed eerily from exit signs above the ladder stairs.

It made me think of Samantha. Was Samantha booted up? Was she connected to the special effects? She must be, at least partly; Josh had been at that for some time. *Connect*, a voice seemed to say in my head, and it was not Samantha, though Samantha had been known to feed me data when I was in Alpha state. This was my own intuition, suggesting I would need to be in that state, and quickly.

I heard a faint swish, like fabric drifting in the breeze, as though the draperies along the walls had stirred. As though a cold finger touched me. There was no breeze. There could be no breeze, here in this sealed room, without a wind machine. And I knew, as surely as though a voice had screamed, that I was not on the grid alone.

I froze, motionless on the walkway, and my heart was pounding. Where should I go? There was no wall to flatten against; I dared not risk exposure on the ladder with its rims of light. *First things first*, I thought, and forced myself to breathe slowly. *Count-four-breathe-in, count-four-breathe-out* . . . my heartbeat and my pulses slowed. *Focus on something still and peaceful . . . my gazebo hideaway beside the lake. . . .* With the relaxed concentration of a cat, I put one shoeless foot before the other, found a position, shifted weight. Again. Again. I was away from the ladder top with its red glow, up to the first intersection of the walkways. I took the right turn. One step, two steps, three.

Then I saw it — sensed more than saw — a solid mass in the darkness, halfway down the next crosswalk. Someone was bending over the two foot pipe. Hands were moving over — what? A C-clamp? I thought I caught a moving glimmer of reflected light. A watch? A ring?

Why had I come up here without a flash-light? Or something with which to protect myself? There was nowhere I could hide, and I dared not risk betraying myself by moving backward toward the ladder rungs. There was one way I could protect myself. *If* everything was in readiness. I kept my gaze on that moving bulk, but I willed my mind's eye to see the gazebo by the lake. My temples throbbed, but my heart and pulse were steady.

SAMANTHA—SAMANTHA—S. O. S. Would she "read" me? She would, if she was booted up, and I was deep enough in Alpha state. *SAMANTHA, GET HELP. SEND JOSH.*

Light glinted again, low near the walkway. The figure was doing something to the grid. I felt the figure straighten. My rational mind, in automatic pilot, clicked through my possibilities. Stay? Retreat? Go forward?

I felt the mass recede. As it did, my right foot shifted forward. *SAMANTHA, GET HELP!* My little toe touched against something cold. A shudder ran through me; I almost lost balance. My left hand went out involuntarily. Caught a stanchion. *GET HELP!* What had my foot touched?

Cautiously, so cautiously, I lowered myself toward the walkway, crouching, still holding the stanchion with my left hand as my right searched carefully. My fingers closed around a shape — small, cold, metal. A wrench. Someone had been tampering with clamps or pipes; the crew obeyed stringent laws against leaving tools around where they could fall and cause harm. Or was that what had been intended?

Carefully, forcing myself not to hold my breath, I drew myself up to full height, and the wrench was in my hand. *Clannng!* . . . it struck against the right hand stanchion.

The air became electric. I felt, rather than saw, the crouching figure swing, and suddenly a flashlight shone full in my eyes. I recoiled, almost fell; caught at the rope railing and righted myself. The beam was brighter . . . closer. . . .

I knew — don't ask me — that something was going to be flung at me, a second before it came. In that second, I ducked. I heard the object whistle past. Before it clattered, far below, I shut my eyes against the blinding light and threw the wrench toward an envisioned target a foot to the right and a foot above its source.

There was a cry, like a wounded animal, and suddenly hands were on my shoulders like a vise. They were at my throat, and the blood thundered in my head, and something somewhere in me screamed, *Don't fight it, use it — like the swimmer and the wave.*

I let myself go limp, heavily, against the other figure, and my right foot came up to hook around a leg. Then we were both falling, as in a lovers' embrace, falling onto the swaying rope, against a stanchion, down onto the narrow walkway and, terrifyingly, over the low pipe. First I was on top, then not, then with skill the figure had flipped sideways and was forcing me out, out over the pipe, out over endless space. And all the while a stream of obscene abuse poured out in that hoarse Celia-voice, and the hands with inhuman strength tore at my throat.

My hands, my arms, fought to force those arms apart and jerk them free. My legs fought to hold the lock they had achieved on the pipe behind. And the voice in my head screamed silently: *S A M A N T H A ! H E L P !*

Suddenly, the blackness was ablaze with light and sound. Colored lights pulsed on and off; strobes swept the grid. Music blared raucously. A huge follow-spot found us; its voltage magnified until it was like the sun.

There was an animal cry, and it was not mine. For a split second, the force that was pitted against me slackened. In that second, everything instinctual in me sprang like a cat. I jerked and twisted, as she had done; pulled myself up on my knees, and brought her with me. I heard her hiss, and felt her gathering to spring. I moved first, flinging myself against her.

It seemed an eternity — it must have been a minute — we hung there over space, like two actors in one of those Ninja movies. And all the while the lights and sound went mad. And then she jerked, and I jerked, and I had the advantage — why, I'll never know. Alpha state? Sanity versus madness? It doesn't matter. What matters is that in the one crucial second *I* twisted sideways, and braced against the stanchion, and she went backward, over the pipe rail, down. Down like a rag doll onto the floor of the sound stage, far below.

The strobe lights stopped their mad careening. The overhead lights sprang on. The melody of Celia's music box theme kept keening through the loudspeakers, as Aunt Jane, the security guards, and actors just arriving swarmed in a shocked circle toward the twisted figure of Margaret Geller, lying there in her last spotlight like a voodoo doll.

It was all so far below. It wasn't real. I crouched on the walkway and could not stop shaking, even when Josh engulfed me in his arms. He had to pry my fingers free of the stanchion, one by one.

Chapter 15

Blessedly, I don't have too much recollection of what happened after that. It zoomed by me, the way Aunt Jane zooms the commercials past when she's watching a back episode on her VCR.

Some individual moments stood out sharp and clear. One was Josh lifting me to my feet and, when he found my legs couldn't hold me, holding me close for a long, long time. I buried my face in his banker's-gray shoulder and clung to him tightly.

"You could have been killed," Josh said hoarsely. "I told you to stay put, but would you listen? Oh, no!" He sounded furious, as he always did when deeply moved.

"You didn't really expect me to sit tight when something was telling me to check the grid *fast*, did you?" I tried to sound calm and collected, but my knees gave away the lie. Josh's arms tightened around me.

"You and your voices! I don't suppose they

told you there was a would-be killer waiting up there, did they? Or did you just take that as a further invitation?"

"I didn't know about — her. Not until I got up there. By then it was a little late." I took a deep breath. "And don't knock my ESP. It got you and Samantha active, didn't it?"

"Samantha freaked out. And you can thank your stars I was in the room with her," Josh said severely. "I still had her case off, but the monitor and her main wiring was hooked up. I was trying to disconnect the circuits, and she darn near electrocuted me!" He stopped, startled. "Come to think of it, she wasn't plugged in! That guy in California said she'd operate on a reserve power system for an hour after being unplugged, didn't he? We'd just never gotten around to trying it."

The "guy in California" was Samantha's inventor; I refrained from pointing out that Josh had doubted Samantha's capacity in this respect as much as he'd once doubted her Alpha capabilities. I asked instead, "What did Samantha do?"

"Burned my fingers, and started spitting colored light rays at me. *Then* she started blinking out, 'GET HELP!' I figured it was you," Josh said unnecessarily, "but I didn't know what was happening where, or how much time I had. So I flipped on the surveillance cameras — thank goodness, I'd just finished getting them connected — and when I saw the two of you struggling —" I felt a shudder run through him; Josh, who prided himself on his control. "I felt so damn helpless!" he burst out. "There was no way I could get up there without being noticed. So I scooped up Samantha, and ran her into the technical room, hooked her to the master fuse board, and told her to do her stuff." He let his breath out. "Thank the Lord, she did."

"She certainly did." I had a vivid picture of Josh, his arms full of the heavy hardware, making the frantic dash. And being Josh, still having the steady hands to do that delicate wiring work. "Josh, the cameras — how did you pick up anything? It was black as pitch up here."

"Infrared cameras. I think of everything, except how to keep you from walking into a trap."

"It wasn't a trap. At least, not until I got up here. *I* trapped *her*." Involuntarily, I glanced down toward the sound stage, and Josh caught my chin in his hand and turned it back away.

"Don't look. You don't want to see."

"I already saw." I willed my voice steady. "Josh, how bad is it?" When he didn't answer, I made myself add, "I — heard her head hit the cement floor."

"She's alive. Was, when I came up here. I didn't wait to hear any more." Josh held me off slightly so he could look at me. "Sidney, did you *know* who it was? I couldn't see faces on the monitor, only forms. Could you tell?"

"I knew who it had to be. That's why I came up. I knew she probably still had a key ... and knew this studio inside and out ... and I'd read stuff about what a whiz she was at lighting. So I figured she'd probably try to rig something before anyone knew she was out of the hospital. That's why I made myself climb that ladder." I glanced toward it and felt very shaky. "I don't know how I'm going to make it back down."

I started to giggle, crazily, and Josh, alarmed, said, "Oh, Lord, don't *you* freak out!" And my laughter, to my own astonishment, turned to tears, and I hung onto Josh's lapels and bawled — until Josh started kissing me, which brought me back to reality in a hurry.

After that, things get foggy. I know I got down the ladder rungs, with Josh going down ahead of me, his left hand on the rungs and his right arm around my waist. I know Aunt Jane, Ross Taylor, and Leslie and her husband, were waiting at the foot. I had a glimpse of Margaret Geller, lying there like a broken doll, with something dark red and sticky trickling from her nose and mouth. Then an ambulance crew was there, with a dark young doctor with sober eyes, and the now-familiar police lieutenant and his colleagues. After that I was firmly parked in the designers' office, along with Josh, with Leslie for support and a policeman to make sure we did not discuss the case. We were supposed to save that for the private sessions the lieutenant was holding with all concerned in Aunt Jane's office, with Jane herself being the first one grilled.

When it came my turn, the whole thing had an unreal air, as if I was watching myself on a TV screen. The lieutenant listened without comment to my account of how and why I'd climbed that ladder, and he didn't look as skeptical as I'd feared. Aunt Jane must have briefed him on my ESP and Alpha, not to mention Samantha, our secret weapon. He did want to know why I'd suddenly been so sure The Joker was Margaret Geller, and if I was so sure, why I hadn't told him.

"I wasn't sure, not until I was sitting out there alone thinking," I said tiredly. "I mean, I thought in the beginning she was the logical person. Motive, and psychology, and all. But then, when she was attacked, I figured it had to be somebody else."

"I know. George Albert Geller. We heard about that." There was an inscrutable twinkle in the lieutenant's eyes. He probably knew a lot more about Josh's computerized fishing expedition than we'd wanted. "For your information, Geller *is* dead. Some time after that case was closed, we succeeded in obtaining his dental records, and they confirmed his identity. Now I asked you, Miss

Webster, what made you so sure again that the perpetrator in this case was Margaret Geller?"

How could I explain my ESP convictions? I couldn't even drag Samantha in on it. "It was the soap opera-ish-ness," I said simply. "Ms. Kirby told you, we've been doing research on successful soaps, and on the past history of this one. One thing the research showed is that writers tend to develop trademarks . . . plot situations, and gimmicks, and character relationships that they use again and again. And also that their art mimics their life, and vice versa. It hit me, how much of what was happening *behind* the scenes here resembled what was happening *on* screen. Love-hate relationships . . . they've always been a Geller trademark, on stage and off. And her pathological attachment to a character that had pathological attachments." I was starting to sound like a psych textbook, maybe because I was so tired.

"Celia, and the resemblance to both Ms. Geller and her daughter." So the lieutenant knew a lot more about *Lust for Life* than than we'd given him credit for.

"And the discovery of Ms. Geller after she'd been gassed. I kept picturing it, and thinking I'd seen it before. And I had — on TV, when Celia's body was discovered."

"She cribbed her escape from the hospital from TV, too." The corners of the lieutenant's mouth twitched slightly. "Sleeping medication spit out into a waste basket, a rolled blanket in the bed. And she calmly walked down the hall, into a storage closet where she helped herself to a white lab coat and clipboard, and out of the hospital. I've seen that stunt used in a dozen hospital shows. And I've torn a strip off the greenhorn who was supposed to guard her door."

"He was there to protect a victim, not guard a suspect, wasn't he?" I noticed that the lieutenant didn't answer. "So he probably didn't think anything of somebody coming *out* of the room, not going *in*. And Margaret Geller was an experienced actress. That's one thing I found out, how good everyone said she'd have been if she'd been in front of the cameras, rather than at a typewriter. She used to demonstrate how she wanted to have scenes played. She could fool anyone. And she could do anything — everything connected with theatrical illusion."

Suddenly, vividly, the struggle on the grid came back to me, and its aftermath. The rest of the interview was one of those things that's a blank.

I think I fainted. I remember somebody bringing me water, and somebody else coffee, and Josh making a scene. And then, crazily, my mother and father were there to drive me home. We rode in silence, Mother and Dad and Josh and me, and Josh and I were holding hands. Aunt Jane wouldn't leave. She was in command at *Lust for Life,* and she would not leave her post.

She telephoned, though, late that evening. The phone woke me, and I listened in on the extension as Aunt Jane and Mother talked.

"She's dead," Aunt Jane said. "She died without regaining consciousness." I heard my mother gasp and, in the background, my father's exclamation.

"I'm here. I heard," I said steadily. "I'm Okay."

"Sidney, don't worry. Do you hear me?" Aunt Jane was very firm. "It was not your fault. The lieutenant says you'll have to make a formal statement, but there's no question that her death was an accident, resulting from her attack on you. Whatever you did, you did in self defense."

"I know." I was proud that I was able to make my voice stay calm. But I could not get back to sleep.

That formal statement was another part of the blur. So was telling — or avoiding telling — all and sundry what had *really* happened. Margaret Geller's death hit the TV morning news in living color (even a shot of her on a stretcher, being carried to the ambulance). It was the first the media had learned of The Joker, and they made the most of it. They cornered Aunt Jane and Leslie Swayne for interviews; both looked haggard but still beautiful, and my whole family noticed that

Ross Taylor was hovering protectively.

Josh, bless him, handled all requests for information — from media and pals — with the double-talk aplomb of a representative of the State Department. Cordelia, who started being agog with curious horror, ended up appointing herself my mother protector. And nobody, thank goodness, as far as we knew, had stumbled onto the fact that Josh and I had gone on hacking expeditions. With the exception, that is, of my father, who favored us with a long lecture on computer ethics and wound up saying it was a good thing *somebody* had found out some of those facts, even if he did not approve of the methods. And that it was a good thing the case had wrapped up satisfactorily before anyone else got hurt.

I do not like the image that comes to mind of myself forcing Margaret Geller out, out across the perilous pipe, until she lost balance and plummeted to lie like a broken doll. Josh understands, probably better than anyone else, because he was there.

No, for me the *real* ending of the case was something that happened several weeks later, after Leslie Swayne had been officially appointed head writer for the show. Josh and I had hand-delivered the thick computer-printouts of our soap research, impressively bound in red leatherette. ("Red for blood," Josh chuckled, then looked as though he wished he hadn't.)

The research had shown that the surefire

attention getters were weddings, violent deaths, spectacular crimes, sizzling love affairs, courtroom trials, and spectacles. "I think we've had enough of violence for at least three months," Aunt Jane said, and proceeded to put her head together with Leslie and Call-me-Jack. The result had been an extragazanza that had Mr. Doyle simultaneously totting up expenses and ratings points. Translated into story line terms, that meant the *very* spectacular wedding festivities of Allison Armitage and Keith Figueroa (who, in the fairy-tale way of soapland, had just been proved to be the missing grandson of a South American oil-and-gold billionaire).

Other shows have had masked balls and costume balls. Leslie Swayne came up with (and the sponsor paid for) an eighteenth-century three-day-long nuptial celebration taking place (supposedly) at newfound grandpa's South American *finca*. Actually, it was filmed on location at a nineteenth-century railroad baron's little place in the center of New Jersey. All the *Lust for Life* characters who had been written out (other than by death) during Margaret Geller's tenure were brought back for the wedding, whenever possible by the actors identified with the roles. And since the Armitage clan, like the South American one, had a far-flung social circle, there was a "cast of thousands" (supposedly flown to South America on private jets by the billionaire) — played by a cast of hundreds, including non-speaking walk-ons by several near-and-dears of the *Lust for Life* company. And Cordelia, and Steve, and Ceegee. And Josh, and me.

Leslie had, brilliantly, managed to corner the ratings race for a good two weeks or more by having *three* wedding ceremonies — a private civil, a lavish cathedral wedding in South America, followed by a "home town" wedding in the "Armitage family church" in the states. (To which, again, the thousands of guests were being privately jetted. Why doesn't anybody ever deal with jet lag in TV scripts?) The "home town" wedding was Edwardian, and the bride wore a point lace gown which had actually belonged to the young actress's own great-great-grandmother. *I* wore *my* great-great-grandmother Palmer's mauve satin dress that she wore to a reception at the White House in 1903. Josh wore a cutaway coat and a false mustache. We looked very spiffy.

But what for me was the real "happy ending" to soap-in-the-afternoon took place earlier, when we all went on location deep in New Jersey for the shots of the South American ball. The white stucco mansion with its heavy beams of carved dark wood was ablaze with candles. Silver and gold and crystal sparkled, and so did the women's jewels and the orders worn by the men. The clothing was tailcoats-and-crinolines, and I felt sorry for Leslie, who could not be in it because her Celia character was so definitely dead. But Leslie, looking on radiantly in a maternity dress she did not yet need, was all serene.

And so was I — if that was the word, when my pulse was racing as Josh and I sashayed in a lively waltz around the ballroom floor. Josh, who never ceased to amaze me, had apparently been taking dancing lessons. The clothing of a diplomat of the 1850's decidedly became him.

I said as much, and he pretended he hated the high collar, but he was pleased. He looked me over, as if through a monocle.

"You should wear those peacock shades more often. They suit you."

Coming from him, that was something. "How about the satins and the crinoline? Better than beat-up slacks and a sweater?" I teased. And then, for an instant, we were both carried back to the terrors of blackness on the lighting grid — me in dark navy, and Margaret Geller all in black.

Josh's hand tightened at my waist. "I've had enough of soap operas to last a lifetime. Let's get out of here," he said.

Behind us Cordelia, enchanting in emerald-green moire, was flirting provocatively with a bemused Steve. Ceegee, in a military uniform he'd managed to rumple, lounged near a gold punch bowl. Aunt Jane, on camera for once, was waltzing in Ross Taylor's arms and despite the dictates of the script, both of them looked as though they were in a dream. Josh and I, arm in arm, went through an archway and out through French doors onto an iron-railed balcony. Off behind the trees, the rosy fingers of dawn were touching New Jersey (pardon me, Peru).

Josh slid his arm around my waist, and I was very conscious of his touch. "Too bad Samantha couldn't be here," I said, striving to be witty.

"Three's a crowd," Josh said calmly. "And I don't give two hoots if the cameras are watching."

And he turned my chin towards him as he had that morning on the grid, and kissed me. And suddenly, the nightmares that had been haunting me were gone . . . replaced by something equally, but far more pleasantly, disturbing.

It wasn't just a happy ending. It was a beginning — of a new stage in SSW Enterprises, and a *whole* lot more.